TRIAL RUN

What Reviewers Say About Carsen Taite's Work

Trial and Error

"Everything I love in Carsen Taite's books is in this one: the law, the flawed characters, the excitement of the plot."—*Jude in the Stars*

Trial by Fire

"Ms. Taite brings something distinctive and special when she writes about law, something that tells her apart from the rest of the lesfic authors. I believe that's when she is at her best. Luckily for me, this is one of those books. ...This novel has the perfect balance between legal thriller and romance. Ms. Taite takes the reader to different legal proceedings and court action, all easy to understand for a layperson like me. It felt a bit like watching a courtroom movie."—*Lez Review Books*

Her Consigliere

"With this sexy lesbian romance take on the mobster genre, Taite brings savvy, confidence, and glamour to the forefront without leaning into violence. ...Taite's protagonists ooze competence and boldness, with strong female secondary characters. ...This is sure to please."—*Publishers Weekly*

"Such a great story! I was literally living for every moment in this. Both Royal and Siobhan were strong, powerful, authoritative women who I was absolutely captivated by. Their worlds and jobs were both edgy and exciting, providing that thrill of a little bit of danger along the way, especially when their emotions and affections for one another started to show. I adored them both and genuinely couldn't get enough of them. They were amazing!"—*LESBIreviewed*

Spirit of the Law

"I'm a big Taite fan, especially of her romantic intrigue books that are about some aspect of the law. She is one of the best writers out there when it comes to writing about courts and lawyers, so when you see a new book of hers in that category, you know you are in for a treat. And a treat is the perfect way to describe what reading Taite's books feel like, like eating a bowl of your favorite Ben and Jerry's ice cream."—*Lezreviewbooks*

Best Practice

"I had fun reading this story and watching the final law partner find her true love. If you like a delightful, romantic age-gap tale involving lawyers, you will like *Best Practice*. In fact, I believe you will like all three books in the Legal Affairs series." —*Rainbow Reflections*

Drawn

"This book held my attention from start to finish. I'm a huge Taite fan and I love it when she writes lesbian crime romance books. Because Taite knows so much about the law, it gives her books an authentic feel that I love. ...Ms. Taite builds the relationship between the main characters with a strong bond and excellent chemistry. Both characters are opposites in many ways but their attraction is undeniable and sizzling."—*LezReviewBooks.com*

Still Not Over You

"*Still Not Over You* is a wonderful second-chance romance anthology that makes you believe in love again. And you would certainly be missing out if you have not read *My Forever Girl* because it truly is everything."—*SymRoute*

Out of Practice

"Taite combines legal and relationship drama to create this realistic and deeply enjoyable lesbian romance. …The reliably engaging Taite neatly balances romance and red-hot passion with a plausible legal story line, well-drawn characters, and pitch-perfect pacing that culminates in the requisite heartfelt happily-ever-after."—*Publishers Weekly*

"*Out of Practice* is a perfect beach read because it's sexy and breezy. There's something effortless about Abby and Roxanne's relationship, even with its occasional challenges, and I loved that I never doubted that they were right for each other."—*Lesbian Review*

Leading the Witness

"…a very enjoyable lesbian crime investigation drama book with a romance on the side. 4.5 stars."—*LezReviewBooks.com*

"…this might be one of Taite's best books. The plotting is solid, the pacing is tight. …*Leading the Witness* is a thrill ride and it's well worth picking up."—*Lesbian Review*

Practice Makes Perfect

"Absolutely brilliant! …I was hooked reading this story. It was intense, thrilling in that way legal matters get to the nitty gritty and instill tension between parties, fast paced, and laced with angst. …Very slow burn romance, which not only excites me but makes me get so lost in the story."—*LESBIreviewed*

Pursuit of Happiness

"This was a quick, fun and sexy read. …It was enjoyable to read about a political landscape filled with out-and-proud LGBTQIA+ folks winning elections."—Katie Pierce, Librarian

"An out presidential candidate (Meredith Mitchell) who is not afraid to follow her heart during campaigning. That is truly utopia. A public defender (Stevie Palmer) who is leery about getting involved with the would-be president. The two women are very interesting characters. The author does an excellent job of keeping their jobs in focus while creating a wonderful romance around the campaign and intense media focus. …Taite has written a book that draws you in. It had us hooked from the first paragraph to the last."—*Best Lesfic Reviews*

Love's Verdict

"Carsen Taite excels at writing legal thrillers with lesbian main characters using her experience as a criminal defense attorney."
—*Lez Review Books*

Outside the Law

"[A] fabulous closing to the Lone Star Law Series. ...Tanner and Sydney's journey back to each other is sweet, sexy and sure to keep you entertained."—*Romantic Reader Blog*

"This is by far the best book of the series and Ms. Taite has saved the best for last. Each book features a romance and the main characters, Tanner Cohen and Sydney Braswell are well rounded, lovable and their chemistry is sizzling. ...The book found the perfect balance between romance and thriller with a surprising twist at the end. Very entertaining read. Overall, a very good end of this series. Recommended for both romance and thriller fans. 4.5 stars."—*Lez Review Books*

A More Perfect Union

"[*A More Perfect Union*] is a fabulously written tightly woven political/military intrigue with a large helping of romance. I enjoyed every minute and was on the edge of my seat the whole time. This one is a great read! Carsen Taite never disappoints!"
—*Romantic Reader Blog*

"Readers looking for a mix of intrigue and romance set against a political backdrop will want to pick up Taite's latest novel."
—*RT Book Review*

Sidebar

"As always a well written novel from Carsen Taite. The two main characters are well developed, likeable, and have sizzling chemistry."—Melina Bickard, Librarian, Waterloo Library (UK)

"Sidebar is a love story with a refreshing twist. It's a mystery and a bit of a thriller, with an ethical dilemma and some subterfuge thrown in for good measure. The combination gives us a fast-paced read, which includes courtroom and personal drama, an appealing love story, and a more than satisfying ending." —*Lambda Literary Review*

Letter of the Law

"If you like romantic suspense novels, stories that involve the law, or anything to do with ranching, you're not going to want to miss this one."—*Lesbian Review*

Without Justice

"This is a great read, fast paced, interesting and takes a slightly different tack from the normal crime/courtroom drama. …I really enjoyed immersing myself in this rapid fire adventure. Suspend your disbelief, take the plunge, it's definitely worth the effort." —*Lesbian Reading Room*

"Carsen Taite tells a great story. She is consistent in giving her readers a good if not great legal drama with characters who are insightful, well thought out and have good chemistry. You know when you pick up one of her books you are getting your money's worth time and time again. Consistency with a great legal drama is all but guaranteed."—*Romantic Reader Blog*

Above the Law

"…readers who enjoyed the first installment will find this a worthy second act."—*Publishers Weekly*

Reasonable Doubt

"I liked everything. The story is perfectly paced and plotted, and the characters had me rooting for them. It has a damn good first kiss too."—*Lesbian Review*

Lay Down the Law

"This book is AMAZING!!! The setting, the scenery, the people, the plot, wow. …I loved Peyton's tough-on-the-outside, crime fighting, intensely protective of those who are hers, badass self."—*Prism Book Alliance*

"I've enjoyed all of Carsen Taite's previous novels and this one was no different. The main characters were well-developed and intriguing, the supporting characters came across as very 'real' and the storyline was really gripping. The twists and turns had me so hooked I finished the book in one sitting."—Melina Bickard, Librarian, Waterloo Library (London)

Courtship

"Taite (*Switchblade*) keeps the stakes high as two beautiful and brilliant women fueled by professional ambitions face daunting emotional choices. …As backroom politics, secrets, betrayals, and threats race to be resolved without political damage to the president, the cat-and-mouse relationship game between Addison and Julia has the reader rooting for them. Taite prolongs the fever-pitch tension to the final pages. This pleasant read with intelligent heroines, snappy dialogue, and political suspense will satisfy Taite's devoted fans and new readers alike."—*Publishers Weekly*

Switchblade

"I enjoyed the book and it was a fun read—mystery, action, humour, and a bit of romance. Who could ask for more? If you've read and enjoyed Taite's legal novels, you'll like this. If you've read and enjoyed the two other books in this series, this one will definitely satisfy your Luca fix and I highly recommend picking it up. Highly recommended."—*C-Spot Reviews*

Battle Axe

"This second book is satisfying, substantial, and slick. Plus, it has heart and love coupled with Luca's array of weapons and a bad-ass verbal repertoire. ...I cannot imagine anyone not having a great time riding shotgun through all of Luca's escapades. I recommend hopping on Luca's band wagon and having a blast."—*Rainbow Book Reviews*

Beyond Innocence

"As you would expect, sparks and legal writs fly. What I liked about this book were the shades of grey (no, not the smutty Shades of Grey)—both in the relationship as well as the cases."—*C-spot Reviews*

Nothing but the Truth

"Taite has written an excellent courtroom drama with two interesting women leading the cast of characters. Taite herself is a practicing defense attorney, and her courtroom scenes are clearly based on real knowledge. This should be another winner for Taite."—*Lambda Literary*

It Should be a Crime—*Lammy Finalist*

"Taite, a criminal defense attorney herself, has given her readers a behind the scenes look at what goes on during the days before a trial. Her descriptions of lawyer/client talks, investigations, police procedures, etc. are fascinating. Taite keeps the action moving, her characters clear, and never allows her story to get bogged down in paperwork. *It Should Be a* Crime has a fast-moving plot and some extraordinarily hot sex."—*Just About Write*

Visit us at www.boldstrokesbooks.com

By the Author

Truelesbianlove.com

It Should be a Crime

Do Not Disturb

Nothing but the Truth

The Best Defense

Beyond Innocence

Rush

Courtship

Reasonable Doubt

Without Justice

Sidebar

A More Perfect Union

Love's Verdict

Pursuit of Happiness

Leading the Witness

Drawn

Double Jeopardy (novella in Still Not Over You)

Spirit of the Law

Her Consigliere

TRIAL RUN

by

Carsen Taite

2024

TRIAL RUN
© 2024 By Carsen Taite. All Rights Reserved.

ISBN 13: 978-1-63555-865-4

This Trade Paperback Original Is Published By
Bold Strokes Books, Inc.
P.O. Box 249
Valley Falls, NY 12185

First Edition: December 2024

Credits
Editor: Cindy Cresap
Production Design: Susan Ramundo
Cover Design By Tammy Seidick

Acknowledgments

Thanks to the entire crew at Bold Strokes Books for giving my stories a home. Huge thanks to my smart, funny, and very patient editor, Cindy Cresap who I'm lucky to call a good friend. Tammy, thank you for the striking covers for this entire series.

Many thanks to my fellow authors and friends in the writing community who offer constant cheerleading and support. The friendships I have made in my writing journey are a big bonus to this career and I cherish them all. Paula, thanks for always being available to be a sounding board, a brainstorm trooper, and the best ride-or-die a pal could hope to have.

Thanks to my wife, Lainey, for always believing in my dreams even when they involve sacrificing our time together. I couldn't live this dream without you, and I wouldn't want to.

And to you, dear reader, thank you for taking a chance on my work and coming back for more. Thanks for taking this journey with me.

Dedication

To L. Always.

CHAPTER ONE

"Get down!"

The barked words cut through the thick smoke, and once again Reggie couldn't tell if the voice was friend or foe, but the sharp repeating loud bangs told her the difference could be deadly. Before she could decide, her shoulder burst into flames, and she looked down in time to see the files she'd been holding flutter to the ground. Stabs of pain ripped through her and she grasped her arm as her knees buckled. Wet, warm—she pulled her hand back and stared at the bright red blood, barely comprehending it was her own right before she dropped to the ground beside the papers she'd held moments ago.

Bang. Reggie shot awake at the sound, unsure if it was real or a tendril from her dream weaving through her real life—an occurrence happening way more often than she'd ever expected. A quick look around the room told her she was safe at home in her bedroom. The nap had seemed like a good idea when her head hit the pillow, but its goal was elusive and she was neither rested nor refreshed, only more stressed than she was when she was awake. She heard another bang, this one lighter, and she recognized the sound of the postman replacing the facing on the group of mailboxes outside her apartment.

Mail. The word amplified her focus, and she threw off the covers and pulled on the sweats she'd tossed on the end of her bed. A moment later, she was standing in front of the bank of mailboxes and she took a deep breath. Every day she'd checked and every day there was nothing more than bills and junk, but maybe today would be different.

Reggie reached a hand up into the mailbox, but a sharp pain caused her to drop the mail onto the ground, echoing her dream. She rubbed her shoulder, silently cursing the effects of her injury which were taking way too long to heal and stared at the letters strewn on the ground. Most of them appeared to be junk, but she bent down and gathered them up, hoping the letter she'd been expecting was tucked in the mess.

It was at the bottom of the stack. She wanted to rip it open right there, but she also wanted to savor the moment, so she walked the short distance to her apartment and juggled the mail in one hand while she fumbled to get the keys in the door. It had been months, and she'd expected her arm to be higher functioning than it was by now, but if the letter she was holding said what she hoped, then her injury would no longer be the focal point of her life. She was long past ready to move on.

She tossed the mail on the kitchen counter and reached into the fridge for a beer because no matter what the letter said, she was either going to want to celebrate or commiserate. What she really wanted was company to share the news, whatever it was, but since she'd left her job at the courthouse, it had become harder and harder to reconnect with the family she'd had there. She'd shown up for a few happy hours to celebrate big wins and birthdays, but increasingly she'd felt like an outsider, not knowing the cases they discussed or the new personnel who'd been hired to take the place of her and others like her, who'd left to pursue other jobs after the shooting. Not for the first time, she felt a pang of guilt for moving on, but the bullet in her shoulder was dedication enough for a lifetime.

She unscrewed the cap on the beer and took a deep pull before reaching for the envelope with the State of Texas official seal. She held it for a moment and closed her eyes, using her dad's favorite technique for making things happen. She envisioned the words inside, saying everything she wanted them to say, and then, unable to control her patience any longer, she tore it open and devoured the letter within.

Congratulations. You've been authorized to sit for the Private Investigator's examination...

There was more, a lot more, about the details of the exam, how to study, what to bring, and where to schedule, but none of that mattered right now. She was ready for her new career, and while it would likely have her back at the courthouse from time to time, she'd no longer be trapped in the building, a waiting target for any madman who decided to seek revenge without caring who he mowed down in his path. Besides, she planned to focus on business fraud, personal injury, divorce—the kind of cases where the worst thing that happened was money changing hands. She clinked her beer bottle against the handle of the refrigerator, a toast to her new life, just as a knock on the door startled her out of her solo celebration.

The face on the other side of the door viewer was her neighbor Evan, the neighborhood gossip. As much as she'd love to have someone to celebrate with, if she invited him in, he would stay for hours. But she knew he'd likely seen her come inside and was unlikely to relent until she answered the door. She eased it open slightly. "Hey, Evan, what's up?"

He peered around her, like he was looking to see who else might be inside, but she kept the opening narrow to thwart his nosy self. Finally, he held up an envelope. "This came for you.

Damn postman put it in my box by mistake." He lowered his voice to a serious-sounding whisper. "Looks important."

Two important letters in one day—what were the odds? She reached for the envelope and he reluctantly let go. When she pulled it toward her, she processed it had an official seal like the other, but this one wasn't from the state of Texas, it was from Dallas County. The courthouse to be precise and she instantly recognized it for what it was. She looked up to see Evan staring at her.

"You going to open it?"

She shook her head. "Not right now." She glanced back into her apartment. "I'm in the middle of something, but thanks for bringing this by." She eased the door shut, knowing she was being rude, but not caring because she wanted to be alone. She walked back into the kitchen and ripped open the envelope only to find her fears confirmed.

You've been summoned to appear for jury duty.

She almost laughed. Of all the reasons she could be pulled back to the courthouse, she never imagined jury duty would be the reason. Given her history, she'd never be selected and the whole ordeal would be a waste of time, but funny, nevertheless. She set down the letter and stared at her phone. One call might make the notice go away, but did she really want to use up a favor on this when there was no chance she'd get picked for a jury anyway?

Nope. She was on a roll right now and a couple of hours at the courthouse spent waiting to be sent home from jury duty wasn't going to bring her down.

❖

"Mom, I hate these."

Brooke looked up from her textbook at her son, Ben, who was wearing his very best ick face while holding a partially eaten donut. She laughed. "No one hates donuts." She cocked her head and frowned. "Are you really my child?"

"I don't hate all of them, but this one." He made a spitting sound. "It's horrible."

"Drama and donuts. That's pretty extra for a Monday morning." Brooke reached out her hand. "Give it to me." She reached for the sticky circle of wonder and took a big bite. The yeasty dough melted on her tongue and her mouth watered as she savored the salty sweet bacon against the maple glaze. She held the rest of the donut in the air, pointing it at her son. "One day, mark my words, you will long for delectables such as these and wish you had enjoyed more of them while you had the metabolism of a twelve-year-old."

"What does that even mean?"

She shook her head, wishing she'd kept her mouth shut. "Never mind. You don't need to worry about anything like that for a very long time." She shoved one of the napkins that had come with the donuts into her book and slammed it shut. "I think I'm ready for my exam. How about you?"

"I guess so. I mean I studied my brains out, but not as much as you."

It was true, she'd studied her brains out for her economics exam, but she wasn't entirely confident her efforts would pay off. She had a basic grasp of the subject, but every time she went to class or reviewed the materials, it felt like everyone was speaking a foreign language. She'd resorted to watching reruns of *Billions* and the movie *Wall Street* to get a basic understanding, but whether either of those crutches would help with the test remained to be seen.

She poured the last bit of coffee in a thermos and motioned for Ben to head to the car while glancing at her watch. She had exactly enough time to drop him off at school and make it to class, but when they barreled out the door, her landlord filled the doorframe. Damn.

"Hi, Mr. Peterson." She mouthed "let me do the talking" to Ben, and shook her head, hoping Peterson wouldn't bring up the past due rent in his presence. "I was going to come see you after work today."

"See that you do," he said with an extra dose of surly. "I won't hold my breath though." He reached into his pocket and pulled out an envelope and she held her breath, praying it wasn't an eviction notice. "The postman just came and he had this letter for you. I told him I'd bring it by." He held it up and squinted. "Looks kind of official."

He shoved it at her, and she took it and stuffed it into her book bag without a second glance, taking a small amount of joy in his crestfallen expression as he realized she wasn't going to share the contents with him. The guy had a lot of nerve, intercepting her mail. No doubt he was hoping it was a big check so she could pay her rent on time. Fat chance.

"Mom, we better get going, right?"

She shrugged away her thoughts about Mr. Peterson and led Ben to the car. When they pulled up to his school, the lack of cars told her they were late. Again. "Sorry, bud."

"It's okay. We missed all the waiting in line this way."

She grabbed his shoulder and squeezed before he jumped out of the car. Some days his positive attitude was the only thing that kept her going. She was a grown-ass woman and shouldn't be relying on an adolescent to keep her sane.

She sighed and shifted her focus to the rest of her day. If she didn't hurry up, she was going to be late to her own exam, and college professors were way less accommodating than middle school teachers.

James, the teaching assistant for Professor Wiles, was passing out the exam as she walked into the room. He shot her the same annoyed glance she'd received many times during the semester, and she slipped into a seat in the back of the room and fumbled through her bag in a quest to find a pen that worked. Her hand brushed the letter Mr. Peterson had brought over and she bent the edge to look at the return address. Dallas County Courts. Definitely not a check. Nothing good came from a court notice. She looked back at the front of the room and saw that James was still several rows in front of her, so she risked a look at the front of the envelope, and her heart stopped when she spotted capital letters in big, bold, red type: JURY SUMMONS.

Crap. One more obligation to navigate in her already overpacked schedule. Single, working moms with a full college load should automatically get a free pass. She started to rip open the envelope to see what hoops she'd need to jump through to make that happen when James's voice hissed in her ear.

"It's a little late to be looking at your notes."

She met his eyes with her most stern mother look and let the frost linger for a full moment before she put the envelope away and accepted her copy of the exam from him. This guy might have all the power right now, but she wasn't about to let him know that. "Thank you, James. I'm sure Professor Wiles is thankful to have someone to handle all his administrative tasks."

He huffed away and she instantly regretted her impulsive act. One day her mouth was going to get her into trouble, and she already had more than she could manage.

Two hours later, she handed in her exam and prayed for the best. She'd finished in the middle of the pack, timing-wise and hoped the grade would be about the same. She needed this course to graduate, but it wasn't going to make her career ambitions. She rushed to her car to find a ticket for having exceeded the time on the meter and she stuffed it in her bag with the jury summons. The law was not on her side today, but she didn't have time to dwell on her misfortune.

A few minutes later, she pushed through the doors at Dante's, the restaurant where she worked. Lunch prep was in full swing and the owner, Lydia, called out for her to head directly to the private room in the back and get it ready for a special reservation. She gladly complied, and used the first few minutes in the empty space to read through the letter from the Dallas County Courts. A quick scan of the possible ways out told her she didn't have a viable excuse and she'd have to show up in person to plead her case, but when she checked the report date, she saw it was for the following Monday morning. How could that be? She'd never gotten a jury summons before, but surely they gave a person more than forty-eight hours' notice before sucking their lives away?

"Why isn't there water on the table?"

Brooke whirled around, startled by Lydia's voice. "Sorry, I just got some bad news. I'm going to need to take Monday off."

"No chance. We've got the Rotary Club lunch and that other thing. I need everyone working all week."

Brooke held up the notice. "Nothing I can do about it. Jury summons."

Lydia laughed. "Seriously? I've gotten four of those and they've all gone directly in the trash." She held her arms out wide. "Don't see me getting thrown in jail, do you?" She smiled. "The cops have better things to do than to hunt down no-shows for snooze duty. Trust me, you'll be fine. Toss it, but for now, focus on your job."

Lydia glided out of the room and Brooke watched her go. Maybe Lydia was right. She could toss the notice just this once. She'd make a promise never to ignore another one. Who would know?

Her phone chose that exact moment to loudly announce a new call with the obnoxious Imperial March ring tone Ben had chosen for his incoming calls. She pulled the phone to her ear without bothering to glance at the screen. "Hey, kiddo. Make it fast, the boss is close by."

"No need to worry. The boss is in her office."

The voice was low and even. Not Ben. No, it was someone else. Someone close by. She glanced around the room, but she was the only one there. She held the phone out an arm's length and looked at the screen. Unknown caller. Had to be a crank call. She moved her thumb toward the red button to hang up but froze at the next words.

"Listen carefully to everything I'm about to say. Ben's life depends on it."

CHAPTER TWO

Reggie watched while the petite woman in front of her hefted her big bag onto the conveyor belt, certain the contents were going to trigger a search. Why would anyone carry a bag that big into the courthouse anyway, especially after what had happened a few months ago. Anyone who barely even watched the news knew about the shooting and the enhanced security that came after.

"Sorry for holding up the line."

The woman tossed the comment over her shoulder, looking back long enough for Reggie to see her flushed cheeks and her brow furrowed into a contrite expression. Okay, no matter how annoyed she was to be standing in this line, she didn't have to be an asshole. She pointed at the bag. "If you have anything in there that's likely to set off the alarm, you're going to want to take it out and put it in one of those trays." She pointed at the dog food bowls that served as the catchall for watches, electronics, etc. that might trigger the metal detector.

"Thanks." She tugged a tablet out of her bag and shoved it into one of the bowls and set it on the conveyor belt.

"First time here?" Reggie asked. The woman was attractive and now that she'd started talking to her, she may as well go all in.

"That obvious?"

"I'm a trained observer." The woman flinched slightly at her words, but the motion registered large on Reggie's radar. She'd hit a nerve. For all she knew, this woman, beautiful or not, might be a defendant in one of the cases being tried this morning. Petite, late twenties to early thirties, business casual except for the very large bag that screamed new mommy or traveling salesperson. Her first guess was potential juror, but that was probably wishful thinking. She could be here for any number of reasons: witness, defendant, consultant, lawyer. Only one way to find out for sure. "What brings you to the courthouse today?"

There it was—the flinch again. Reggie doubted anyone else nearby would've noticed it, but she was clear about what she'd seen, and this woman would rather be anywhere else but here, and she really, really wanted to know why.

No, you don't. You'd just rather be playing detective than be stuck in this building listening to the work of some other investigator who probably didn't do as good of a job as you could.

The woman glanced around furtively. "Jury duty." She whispered the words, and her voice was tinged with anxiety.

Reggie smiled encouragingly. "Me too. Sucks, right?" She looked around to make sure no one else was in earshot, and deciding it was safe to be honest, she added, "And a total waste of time since no one's going to let me on their jury."

The woman's eyes narrowed, and Reggie instantly regretted the overshare. Before the woman could ask any questions, she backed away and pointed toward a crowd of people across the lobby. "I see someone I know. It was nice to meet you." She turned before the woman could reply. Of course, she had to meet an attractive woman at the courthouse—the last place she wanted to be.

She cut through the crowd waiting for the elevators and slipped into the stairwell. Judge Aguilar's courtroom was on the seventh floor, a climb she used to scale with ease, but today she was winded when she emerged into the hallway. Damn, she was more out of shape than she realized. She took a moment to catch her breath before entering the DA workroom just outside of the courtroom. Lennox Roy rose to greet her. "Hey, Reggie. I knew you couldn't stay away for long."

"As if." She reached into her pocket and pulled out the jury summons. "Pretty sure this is the only thing that could bring me back here."

Lennox took the paper, skimmed the first few lines, and laughed. "Like anyone's going to let you on a jury."

"That's what I said. You think Judge Larabee would get rid of this for me?"

"Maybe if you hadn't waited until today. They've got lots of cases teed up and ready today and with the Benton trial starting, they're going to run short on jurors. Plus, you know how he is."

She did. She'd been Judge Larabee's court coordinator for years and seen him shrug off tons of worthy excuses for not being able to serve—way better than her simple "don't want to be here" offering. His theory was everyone should serve on a jury at least once in their lives and with a scarce pool to pick from, it wasn't the day to test his resolve. "Guess I'm doomed to be here until lunch then."

"Maybe they'll cut you loose on a mid-morning break. Have you taken your exam yet?"

Lenox had been the one to suggest private investigation work might be a good next career. She'd get to use many of the skills she'd honed at the courthouse but set her own schedule and decide what cases she wanted to take on. Control, or the semblance of it anyway, was her primary focus, and she'd do whatever she needed to do to get back to it. "The exam's in two weeks. I'll be ready." She waved the summons in the air. "Assuming this doesn't trip me up."

"Well, at least you know you won't get picked for the highest profile case starting today."

"True." She stared hard at Lennox, trying to get a read on her mood. "You okay?"

"I'll be glad when it's over." She reached over and clasped Reggie on the arm. "You will be too."

At that moment, the door to the workroom flew open and Wren, Lennox's girlfriend, burst in. "Hey, Reggie." She stopped and gave her a hug before slipping an arm around Lennox. "You doing okay?"

"Why does everyone keep asking me that?"

"I don't know. Maybe because the man who tried to kill us all and set Lennox's brother up to spend twenty years in prison is finally going to get what's coming to him." She hunched her shoulders. "Maybe my feelings are still a little raw on the subject."

Reggie rubbed her arm while Wren spoke. It was phantom pain—she knew as much, but it didn't mean the memory of the day a shooter opened fire in the courtroom only steps away didn't burn as much. She'd known Harry Benton's trial was starting today, but she blocked it from her consciousness. He hadn't pulled the trigger, but he was as responsible for sending her life spiraling down a different path as much as the gunman who'd burst into the courtroom last fall, and she still couldn't process how that made her feel.

She shook her head. Now was not the time to start getting gushy about it—her constant mantra and the one keeping her focused enough to start her new career. She just had to get out of here first. "I'm good."

"And she's here for jury duty," Lennox said, "So no tainting the pool with your inflammatory proclamations."

Wren laughed. "As if anyone would believe I'm in here pushing a prosecution agenda." She was the rising star in the public defender's office and passionate about protecting the rights of the accused. "Besides, no way would Reggie wind up on Benton's jury. Even his attorneys aren't that dumb."

"I'm counting on not winding up on any jury." Reggie pointed at her watch. "Every minute here is time away from studying for the exam." She looked at the time. "Have you seen Judge Aguilar? I've only got a few minutes before I have to be downstairs, but I figured I'd say hello."

"She's got a hearing on a bond motion this morning, but I'll let her know you're here. If you get a chance to stop by before you leave, I'm sure she'd love to see you."

"Will do." Reggie hesitated a second before turning to leave, an invite to grab a beer at the end of the day on the tip of her lips, but Lennox's face was back on her files and Wren was deep into negotiations with one of the other prosecutors in the workroom. In a few minutes, they'd all be in the courtroom for hearings, pleas, and other business, none of which she had a part in anymore. It had been her choice to leave, but standing in the thick of it, she couldn't help but wonder who she was now and if she'd made a colossal mistake.

The elevators were crammed, smelly, and slow, and Brooke wished she were anywhere but this place. Or that she were more like her boss, Lydia, a woman secure in her job and confident enough to toss a jury summons in the trash like it was another offer for a better cable rate.

But she wasn't Lydia. She was a broke, single mother slash college student, desperate to make a good life for her son which, above all things, meant keeping him alive.

She reached into her bag and let her fingers trace the edge of the envelope delivered the evening after she'd received the ominous phone call. The thin envelope contained a card decorated with letters cut out from magazines, serial killer style. *His life depends on you. More to come.*

Creepy yes, but mostly terrifying. She'd carried it with her at all times since it had appeared, determined to keep Ben from seeing it, while vacillating about what to do about it. This was the point in the movies when all the viewers thought the person being blackmailed, ransomed, or threatened in any way should go straight to the cops and then issued a collective groan when the "hero" decided to go it on their own. She was no hero, but she wasn't dumb either, and the voice on the phone hadn't been messing around. Whoever it was knew things about her. Things that were personal and private, and if they had taken the time and trouble to know those things, they could make good on the threat to harm her son.

"You should take the stairs."

She whirled around, startled at the voice breaking into her thoughts. It was the woman from the security line. The very attractive, very friendly woman. Brooke stiffened. Maybe a little too friendly. Was this woman following her? Was she an innocent bystander or was she the in-person eyes, working on behalf of the guy on the phone? "What are you doing here?"

"Excuse me?"

Damn. Now this woman was going to think she was crazy. She ran her fingers over the card in her bag. She might very well be crazy, but if she was going to make it through this ordeal she needed to pull herself together. "Sorry, you surprised me." She looked around. "And I'd definitely take the stairs if I knew where they were."

The woman motioned over her shoulder. "Come on, I'll show you the way." She took a step, paused, and looked back. "I'm Reggie, by the way."

"I'm Brooke. Nice to meet you, Reggie, tour guide to jurors everywhere."

"Let's not get carried away." Reggie grinned. "I'll start with you and see how it goes."

Her friendly manner was infectious, and Brooke decided to trust her. For now. She followed her through the throng of people, down the hall to a nondescript door, but when Reggie held it open for her, she hesitated.

"What's the matter?"

So many things, most of which had to do with the dangers of following a stranger through an unmarked door in an unfamiliar building, but saying any of those things out loud felt even more dangerous. Her thoughts scrambled to find something innocuous to say and she blurted out the first thing that surfaced. "Are you supposed to wear jeans for jury duty?"

Reggie looked down at her clothes and back again, wearing the grin from before. "Probably not, but I don't plan to be here for long today." She motioned to the stairs. "Are you coming?"

Brooke wanted to ask what Reggie meant about not being here long, but caution told her not to engage, no matter how much Reggie's calm and steady presence tempted her to shed her worry. She glanced back over her shoulder and made a split-second decision. If Reggie was teamed up with whoever it was that wanted her here so desperately, they wouldn't do anything to keep her from the courtroom where she'd been assigned. And if Reggie was nothing more than a kind person offering to help her out, then following her up a few flights of stairs wouldn't hurt anyone. "Lead the way."

A few minutes later, they emerged onto the sixth floor and threaded through another crowd of people to stand outside the courtroom. Reggie exchanged a few words with the uniformed officer standing by the door who then handed them each a clipboard and pen.

"Hold onto these until we call your number," he said.

Brooke skimmed the questions on the clipboard and her heart started to race. She had to wind up on this jury, but she'd had no guidance about how to answer the questions to ensure that would happen. She looked around as if the answers might miraculously appear in the faces of the other people waiting, but the only person who made eye contact with her was Reggie, and her smile, while strangely comforting, didn't tell her what she needed to know.

She took a deep breath and started writing. She'd tell the truth and hope for the best.

CHAPTER THREE

The second row wasn't safe, but it was better than the first.

Reggie walked to the end of the row and remained standing until the rest of the jury panel had filed into the room, mentally counting the consequences of being juror number fifteen. The defense and the prosecution each had six strikes they could use for pretty much no reason, which meant she had to be in the twenties to feel truly safe from being selected, but she was still confident she'd be cut loose soon.

She spotted Brooke in the number two spot. Brooke clearly didn't want to be here either, but seated where she was, she was likely going to wind up in the box. Too bad for her since sitting in this room for days would only ramp up her already present anxiety. Reggie's detective brain kicked in. Brooke's anxiousness felt like more than a case of "I don't want to be stuck on a jury." While she was curious about the source, more than that, she was drawn to this woman. It had been forever since she'd had a date. Maybe if they both got cut by lunchtime…

She shoved the thought aside. If she got cut—make that when she got cut, she needed to get the hell out of here and get back to studying. Lunch with a pretty woman, no matter how intriguing, would only be a distraction.

To keep her mind off Brooke, she scanned the front of the room. The prosecutor was Johnny Rigley, but she didn't recognize his number two. The defense attorney was the infamous Gloria Leland whose clients were usually big local names, but the woman sitting next to her only looked vaguely familiar—middle-aged, white woman with overly styled hair wearing a suit that probably cost more than Reggie had made in a month when she worked at the courthouse.

"All rise," Leroy, the bailiff, called out. Everyone in the room scrambled to their feet as Judge Foster Hunt emerged from a door behind the bench and took his seat.

"Please be seated," he said. "Thanks for being here today." He smiled. "I realize you didn't have a choice, but we appreciate your service nevertheless."

He launched into the usual introductory remarks, pointing out the prosecutor and the defendant and his attorneys who all stood up again. "This case involves an accusation of fraud. Mr. Rigley, representing the state of Texas, is tasked with proving that Ms. Mitchell, represented by Ms. Leland, committed fraud against the citizens of Dallas County by making false statements in order to secure tax breaks and government funding for a development project. Does anyone know Shirley Mitchell?"

Ah, now Reggie knew where she'd seen the defendant's name. Mitchell had been arrested last year for some kind of investment scam. She didn't remember much about the case—so many developers and public officials seemed mired in bribery accusations, she'd lost track of which scheme Shirley's arrest had been part of. Several jurors had hands in the air and the judge called on them one by one.

"Mr. Rodriguez. How do you know Ms. Mitchell?"

"My sister lives in one of her complexes." He hunched his shoulders. "She seems to like it okay."

His tepid review elicited a laugh from the rest of the jurors on the panel and a big fat, fake smile from Shirley Mitchell. Score one for the defense.

Gloria Leland rose from her chair. "Your Honor, if I may."

"Briefly." Judge Hunt didn't even glance at Rigley before he spoke. Reggie hadn't been on a jury before, but she'd witnessed plenty of voir dires, and without exception they started with the judge making a few remarks and then handing the proceeding over to the prosecution and then the defense. Gloria Leland was known for her snake oil salesman brand of charm, but she wouldn't have expected Judge Hunt to fall for her act. Rigley shot daggers at Gloria, but her attention was fully focused on Mr. Rodriguez. "I'm gratified to hear that your sister has access to excellent housing options. Can you tell me what she likes most about where she lives?"

Rodriguez straightened in his chair and beamed at the attention. "I'm not too proud to say that she was happy to find an affordable place to live. Rents are sky-high in the city and landlords are pushing people out every day so they can charge more money. People like my sister can't afford to live near where they work and it's a damn shame."

He shot a look at the judge like he expected to be admonished, but Hunt hadn't flinched at the choice of words. Reggie had seen the judge cuss up a storm when he was pissed off about something going wrong in his courtroom so the simple "damn" probably hadn't fazed him. What had her curious was the speech Rodriguez had delivered. It almost felt like he was a plant designed to get the jury focused on a particular angle Leland was going to push during trial.

As if he had the same thought, Johnny Rigley stood and addressed the judge. "I'm glad we all got to hear what Mr. Rodriguez had to say, but if you're finished with your portion of voir dire, may I have an opportunity to talk to the panel at this time?"

Hunt looked surprised at the question and waved a hand. "Sure, ask away. Each side has one hour."

Rigley cleared his throat and focused on Rodriguez. "Thank you for your candor. I think everyone here would agree with you that affordable housing is important. Right?" He waited a beat while most of the people on the panel raised their hands in assent. "But you'd also agree that affordable housing should come from sound business practices rather than cheating the taxpayers, right?"

Rodriguez shot an apologetic look at Leland. "Well, sure. I mean no one likes to get cheated."

"I agree with you, a hundred percent," Rigley said. "And we're here today to make sure anyone who cheats the citizens of Dallas County is held accountable. Raise your hands if you agree."

Reggie felt silly, but she raised her hand with the others to keep from drawing attention to herself. She'd seen this game enough to know how it was played. Each side doing their best to indoctrinate the panel while ferreting out those who would lead them in a direction other than the one they wanted to go. Normally, silence increased the chances of being selected, but in her case she was betting on silence to keep her from getting selected to serve. Her best chance was to lie low and rely on her former employment here at the courthouse to be the reason her name wasn't called when it came time to seat the jury in the box.

Rigley picked up a piece of paper from counsel table and gazed at the front row of jurors before focusing on Brooke. "Ms. Dawson, what do you do for a living?"

Reggie watched closely, already sensing Brooke's anxiety at being the center of attention. Brooke squirmed in her seat and didn't make eye contact with Rigley. "I'm a student and I have a full-time job."

"It's sometimes hard to make ends meet?"

"Sometimes."

"Affordable housing is probably something important to you."

"I would imagine it's important to anyone who isn't a millionaire."

Reggie smiled at the slight edge in Brooke's tone and the twitter of laughter from the rest of the jurors. Brooke wasn't simply a bundle of nerves—she had spunk.

"True, true," Rigley said. "I imagine you work hard for what you earn."

"I do."

"And you do good, honest work."

"I do my best."

"Thank you." He moved on to the rest of the jurors in the first row, asking questions about their work, following the same general line of implying that they earned their livings doing honest work, and implying Shirley Mitchell did anything but. His method was tried and true, but a little boring and by the time it was Gloria Leland's turn to ask questions, more than a few people on the panel were yawning.

"Well, that was quite the display," Gloria said in a loud voice as she rose again to address them. "Let's summarize. You all think it's a bad idea to earn a living cheating others. Raise your hand if you agree."

Hands shot up across the room and Gloria smiled. "Thank you for that quick and clear answer. Now we move on to the stuff that matters, but before I do, let me assure you that my client, Ms. Mitchell, agrees with you. The question we're here to answer is whether she cheated to get the city contract. Did she bribe a city official? Did she lie in her bid to get the work? The answer to both those questions is no and after the state has presented their case, I have no doubt you will agree that's the case. In fact, I doubt I'll have to do much at all to convince you otherwise once the state is done. How many of you think I or Ms. Mitchell have to prove anything at all?"

A couple of hands shot up and Reggie was certain the response was more about trying to get off the jury than failure to pay attention during high school civics. She let her mind wander while Gloria grilled jurors about whether they were really willing to ignore both the judge's instructions and the Constitution. Meanwhile, Brooke sat perfectly still, facing the front of the room, her eyes trained on the wall. If she worked a couple of jobs to make ends meet, she probably wanted to get out of here as much as anyone else in the room, yet she hadn't volunteered an answer to any question that wasn't directed her way. Didn't she know that sitting quietly was a sure-fire way to ensure she wound up on the jury?

"And what about you, Ms. Knoll?"

Crap. She had no idea what Leland had asked, and she hated having to ask since it made her look like she hadn't been paying attention. She'd been paying attention, just not to her. "I'm sorry, can you repeat the question?"

"You don't think Ms. Mitchell has to prove she's innocent, do you?"

"No, she doesn't."

"Care to expand on that?"

Reggie shrugged. "Not really."

Gloria squinted at her like she didn't believe what she was hearing. "I'm surprised. I thought with your background here at the courthouse, you'd have more to add."

Boom. There it was—her get out of jury duty free card. It was a classic move—out one of the jurors for whatever they were—cop, lawyer, doctor, accountant—use them to make some points in front of the rest of the crowd and then strike them so they couldn't taint the rest of the jurors who wound up serving. Fine. She could play this game. "It's pretty simple, actually. The burden of proof is on the prosecution and the defendant has the right to present a defense or say nothing at all—whichever choice he," she paused and added, "or she makes cannot be considered as evidence to be used against them."

"Well said." Leland turned from her to find her next victim, and when she did, Reggie spotted Brooke staring directly at her with an expression somewhere between surprised and impressed. She smiled in Brooke's direction and Brooke smiled hollowly back. It wasn't much, but it was something.

❖

She couldn't decide if Reggie kept looking at her because she was assigned to make sure she followed the instructions from the phone or if Reggie was interested in her for personal reasons unrelated to jury duty. She wasn't sure she'd even recognize if a woman was interested in her without a flashing sign and a big brass band. It had been that long. Still, there was some spark between them—that was undeniable. Not that it mattered.

Her instructions had been clear. *Answer only direct questions. Do not talk and mingle with the other jurors. More details to follow.* She spoke a silent message to whoever might be watching to let them know that Reggie had approached her, not the other way around.

Thankfully, Gloria finished up her questions without including her in the interrogation. The judge called a recess and she filed out of the room with everyone else.

"Are you going to play hooky if you get cut loose or do you have to go in to work? If it's hooky, what do you think about grabbing lunch?"

Reggie's question was a loaded one and Brooke treaded carefully. "Hooky sounds great, but work is the smart move. For me anyway."

"Too bad. I suppose I'll be left to my own devices."

Brooke titled her head. "What makes you so sure you won't be on this jury? Is it because you used to work here?"

"Yep. Defense won't want me because they think I'll be too sympathetic to crime victims. Prosecutors would've loved to have me on the jury, but…" The words trailed off and she shook her head. "Anyway, I expect to be cut loose when we go back in there. You probably would be too if you'd spoken up a bit more."

Brooke ignored the dig disguised as advice, and wondered what Reggie had been about to say before she changed the subject. If circumstances were different, she'd ask a few questions, get to know her, maybe even invite her to lunch. But her situation was dire. There would be no free afternoon, even if she didn't have a job, homework, and a preteen waiting. She'd be on this jury and she wasn't about to trust anyone else who was. The voice on the phone said she was being watched and she knew it could be anyone in the courtroom, even another juror.

Besides, even without the looming threat, she wasn't in any position to get to know anyone new. Lunch out wasn't a luxury she could afford, and no one wanted to try to work dates around her manic life. She didn't want to have to answer the questions that would inevitably come about how she wound up single and raising a child on her own. Being stuck on this jury would save her from all of that, and maybe that was a good thing.

The bailiff pushed through the courtroom doors and strode into the hallway. "Judge is ready for y'all. You can go in and take a seat wherever you want."

He disappeared back into the room and everyone in the hallway followed, packing the rear rows first. Brooke walked past them all and headed back up the first row. May as well make it easy to get to the jury box when her name was called. She sat down and glanced to her left to see Reggie settling in next to her. "I figured you'd be in the back row, ready to make a break for it."

Reggie grinned. "I may know a secret way to exit."

"You seem to know a lot of things."

"You say that like it's a bad thing."

Warning bells went off at the flirty tone in Reggie's voice, and Brooke shifted gears. "Not at all. It was only an observation." She opened her purse and pretended to look for something inside in a lame maneuver to get Reggie to focus on something besides her. For all she knew, the person who'd called her was watching her right now and might get suspicious that she was being friendly with a stranger. Reggie took the hint and surreptitiously pulled out her phone and started flipping through the contents. She should be relieved not to have to engage any longer, but instead she only felt sad and lonely.

The judge walked into the room and everyone started to get up until he motioned for them to stay seated. "Thanks for your patience," he said. "We're about to wrap up for most of you. The bailiff is going to read the names of those who have been selected to serve and then the rest of you will be free to go." He handed a piece of paper to the bailiff who walked to the center of the room and waited until all eyes were on him.

"When I read your name, come on up here and take a seat in the box." He hitched his pants and studied the paper. "Abigail Dearlove." He waited until she was on her way to the front of the room before reading the next name. "Mark Landon."

He continued the same pattern—name, pause, name, pause—and with each new name he read that wasn't hers, Brooke let out a breath, half relieved and half terrified not to hear her own. What would it mean if he didn't read her name? Was the deal off or would she be held responsible for not fulfilling her end of the bargain? She didn't want to be chosen, but she had to be chosen. Pain enveloped her and she held out her hand to find tiny, red, half moons forming where she'd dug her nails into her palm.

"Regina Knoll"

She heard the gasp from Reggie and whipped her head around in time to see the look of astonishment on her face before she rose and started her slow march to the jury box. If Reggie had been certain she wouldn't be on the jury and she'd been picked, what was to guarantee she, who had to serve, would wind up where she needed to be? What number were they on anyway?

"Raul Rodriguez."

The guy whose sister lived in one of Shirley Mitchell's complexes. Interesting. Brooke watched as he stood and started walking to the front of the room, and then started counting the number of jurors who'd already been selected. Rodriguez would make twelve. She hadn't been picked and she started to panic. She needed to get out of here. Get to Ben's school and make sure he was safe and stayed that way. If the threatening caller reached out again, she'd have to make sure they understood she hadn't done anything to avoid serving and it wasn't her fault their grand plan hadn't worked out.

She looked back at Rodriguez who was only halfway up the aisle. He stopped and grabbed the back of the row in front of him for balance, but his face was ashen, and she could hear the labored breathing from across the room.

"Mr. Rodriguez, are you okay?" the judge asked, his face reflecting genuine concern.

"Sure, Your Honor. Just a little out of breath." With those words, his knees buckled, and he wilted to the floor. The bailiff rushed up the aisle and held everyone back.

"Give him some space." He pointed at two big guys in the closest aisle. "You two, help me get him up."

Brooke watched, stunned like the rest of the panel, while they carried him toward a door in the back of the room. The judge lightly rapped his gavel to get their attention. "While we check on Mr. Rodriguez, please wait here in the courtroom. Counsel, I'd like to see you all in chambers."

As he and the lawyers walked out of the room, Brooke contemplated her options. Now might be the perfect time to duck out. But what if whoever was keeping an eye on her was here in the courtroom? She glanced around. No one seemed to be paying particular attention to her, but when she looked back toward the front of the courtroom Reggie was staring directly at her with her eyebrows drawn in close. Crap. She never should've made eye contact—now she'd missed her chance.

It didn't matter anyway since Judge Hunt and the attorneys chose that moment to walk back into the room. Both sides looked stressed, which was to be expected, and the judge was somber. He asked for everyone's attention and waited until the room was still.

"I'm sorry to say that Mr. Rodriguez will not be able to carry out his duties with us today. That said, we will be continuing to trial." He looked over at the court reporter who sat posed and ready to type. "Taking into account the preemptory strikes already entered by both the prosecution and defense, the next person in line to be selected is Brooke Dawson. Ms. Dawson, please join the rest of the jurors in the box."

Brooke's stomach clenched, but she rose and started walking toward the front of the room, acutely conscious everyone's eyes were on her. She shouldn't be surprised by this development since she'd come here fully expecting to serve. Yet, she'd let herself hope it was all an unfortunate misunderstanding, never intended for her.

She slid into the only open seat that happened to be right next to Reggie. While she tried to wrap her mind around the fact she was stuck here and part of some crazy plan, completely too out of her control, Reggie leaned over and whispered in her ear.

"Guess we get to have that lunch after all."

CHAPTER FOUR

R eggie led the way to the cafeteria in the basement of the building wondering what the hell had just happened. In what world did both the prosecution or defense leave a shooting victim and a courthouse employee on the jury of a criminal case? Yeah, okay, she was a *former* courthouse employee, and this case didn't involve any violence, but still. She was a wild card and attorneys hated those. They liked nice quiet people who could be cajoled into the verdict they wanted and who wouldn't shake things up in the jury room. Then again, these attorneys had let Mr. Rodriguez on the jury despite his overly enthusiastic contributions during voir dire.

The trial was supposed to last a full week, maybe two, which meant she was going to have to pull a bunch of all-nighters if she was going to be ready for her licensing exam. The only upside to this gig she could see was the fact she'd spend the next week or two in close proximity to Brooke. She turned to make sure Brooke was still behind her. Judge Hunt had only given them an hour to grab lunch. "Food here is simple, but good. Plus, by the time you get your car out of the parking garage and drive to the closest place, you'd barely have time to eat before you have to head back."

"Once again, I defer to your tour guide skills," Brooke said, and Reggie spotted a hint of a smile. Rare, but powerful with promise. Brooke Dawson, juror number twelve, could definitely be a distraction. She'd have to be very careful not to let that happen.

"Hey, I think that woman over there is trying to get your attention."

Brooke pointed over Reggie's shoulder and Reggie turned to see Judge Aguilar at a nearby table.

"Um, I'm going to go over and say hello. I'll be right back."

She hesitated for a moment and Brooke waved her away. "It's all good. I promise I can get my own lunch. I'll save you a seat."

Reggie reluctantly edged away and walked over to the judge's table. She'd been filling in as a court coordinator for Judge Aguilar on the day of the shooting and they'd bonded over the experience, but the same circumstance that bound them together also made it painful to be in Nina's presence. Proximity provoked memories and she'd rather forget.

"Hi, Judge."

"Hi, Reggie." She pointed to the empty chair across from her. "Have a seat."

She eyed the chair, scrambling for an excuse, any excuse why she couldn't take a moment to sit across from her old boss and catch up, but nothing came. She slid into the chair but stayed on the edge of the seat. "It's good to see you, Judge."

"It's good to see you too, but 'judge,' really? After everything, I think Nina will do just fine."

"Okay, Judge." Reggie ignored Nina's eye roll. No one called judges by their first name at the courthouse—it was a sign of respect she planned to observe even if they had endured a shooting together.

"Are you here for Benton's trial?"

Reggie shook her head. "As much as I'd like to see him rot in prison for the rest of his life. I'm not sure I'm up for that. What about you? Are you watching any of it?"

"Can't." Nina took a sip of her drink. "I'm getting called as a witness."

Of course. When Benton was in fear the police were on to him for hiring a gunman to shoot up the courthouse in an attempt to kill off his daughter's boyfriend, he'd shown up at Nina's house and tried to intimidate her into calling off the investigation. Instead, she'd chosen to press charges and the DA's office had gladly complied. Their investigation led them to look into his business ventures as well. "Sorry, that was a dumb question."

"It wasn't dumb at all." Nina's eyes were kind. "The whole thing is stressful. I hear his defense plan is to say that he merely came to my house to talk to me and the stress of losing his daughter caused him to be overly emotional. Supposedly, I overreacted to his veiled threats." She rolled her eyes. "I only hope the jury doesn't buy into his charm."

"Speaking of jury duty, I don't suppose you have any pull to get me out of it? I just got picked for a case in Judge Hunt's court."

"Lucky you. If you'd come and seen me before voir dire, I might've been able to help you out, but I wouldn't be inclined to. The parties are lucky to have you." She cocked her head. "Although, I have to say I'm surprised one of them didn't strike you."

"Same. I have no idea how I got through, but I've got my PI licensing exam coming up and jury duty wasn't in the plan. It's Shirley Mitchell's case and it's going to take at least a week. They wound up adding an alternate and you know what that means."

Nina laughed. "It's more likely they picked an alternate because one of the original jurors collapsed in the middle of the courtroom than they were hedging their bets one of you won't last for a long trial, but you didn't hear that from me."

Reggie had figured it didn't hurt to make one last ditch for freedom, but Nina was right. The trial would probably only last a week, and she would survive. Thinking about the case reminded her that Brooke was likely sitting by herself somewhere in the cafeteria. She pushed back her chair and stood. "I need to get going, but it was good to see you. You're a good judge and an even better person, and I hope Benton gets what's coming to him."

"Me too. And good luck with your exam. If you ever decide to come back here to work, I'm sure Lennox would hire you at the DA's office in a heartbeat."

Reggie nodded because saying "when hell freezes over" wasn't polite. She checked her watch, and seeing they only had thirty minutes before they needed to report back, she grabbed a ready-made sandwich and chips and went in search of Brooke. It didn't take long. She was seated at a table with two other women who were also on the jury, one of whom Reggie recognized as having tousled with Gloria Leland about whether the defendant in a case had to prove they were innocent. Lovely. She briefly considered bailing because she wasn't in the mood to socialize with strangers and Brooke obviously didn't need a babysitter, but before she could edge away, the guilty until proven innocent juror waved her over.

"Hi," she said. "I'm Jenny Paulson and this is Lisa Martinez. Brooke said you were busy talking, but we saved you a seat." Jenny looked at Reggie's sandwich. "You should probably eat that fast. We have to be back soon. Was that one of the lawyers who works here that you were talking to?"

Great. In addition to butchering the law, Jenny was a busybody. Reggie took a big bite of her sandwich which allowed her to ignore the question for now. While she chewed the bite, she looked at the other woman, Lisa. She didn't remember a thing about her from voir dire and she'd likely wound up on the jury because she'd kept her mouth shut. Fine by her. If everyone on the jury kept their mouths shut, they'd all be out of here as quickly as possible. "I was talking to someone I knew when I worked in the building. What do you do?"

Jenny launched into a long speech about how she used to work as a very important administrative assistant for a very important businessman, but now she was a greeter at Walmart because it gave her more time for her hobbies and hanging out with her grandkids, but how her job was still very important. Reggie nodded like she cared, but she resented not being able to talk to Brooke one on one, which was the only reason she'd suggested lunch. She caught Brooke's eye, and got a semi-sympathetic expression, but didn't get a feel for whether Brooke either enjoyed Jenny's company or wanted to stick a knife in her brain like she did. Whatever. It was stupid to think she could develop anything out of the whiff of chemistry between them. They were there to hear the evidence and decide a verdict. Anything else was a distraction and she'd had enough of those to last a lifetime.

❖

The defense attorney gave a rousing opening statement, but Brooke still felt her eyelids flickering shut off and on and she was frightened she was going to fall asleep any minute. When Gloria Leland finished and the judge ordered a brief recess, Brooke silently thanked all that was holy. Once they made it back to the jury room, she grabbed her purse and headed to the bathroom with a solid plan to splash water on her face in hopes it would wake her up so she could make it through the rest of the afternoon.

Once there, she set her purse on the counter where it clunked against the surface. Noting it had seemed heavier than usual, she reached a hand in and pulled out a rock the size of a softball.

It had a Post-it attached and the note was spelled out with the lettering she'd come to dread.

Counting on you to weigh things down.

She was on her fifth reading of the note when the door to the bathroom burst open and Jenny and Lisa walked in, laughing and talking. She quickly shoved the rock back in her purse and abandoned her cold water wake-up plan.

"Hey, Brooke," Jenny said. "Are you as sleepy as we are?" She mimicked a yawn. "I hope the rest of the day isn't this boring."

Brooke managed a feeble smile and headed for the door. "Just trying to make it through." It was vague, but true. She pushed through the door and ran smack into Reggie who was standing outside. "Are you following me?" The words tumbled from her lips unbidden, but now that they were out, she wondered if it was true. Reggie was always right freaking there. She could've put the rock in her purse. She could be the eyes in the room reporting back to whoever was hell-bent on her being on this jury. She had no idea if her thoughts made sense, but she was too freaked out to care.

"What?"

She stared into Reggie's eyes. If Reggie was involved in whatever was going on, she was really good at hiding it. Well, except for the always being right there part. Even so, she appeared to be genuinely friendly and helpful. But wouldn't someone who was diabolical have a knack for seeming sincere? But when would she have been able to place the rock in her purse? It hadn't been there before they'd gone into the courtroom after lunch and Reggie had been with her the entire time. Maybe she was losing her mind.

"Never mind." She stepped away, but before she could get far, Reggie reached out and touched her arm. She flinched slightly and Reggie backed up.

"Sorry. I didn't mean to offend you, but I can tell something's going on. Do you want to talk?"

She did, but she couldn't. And even if she could, she couldn't talk to someone she barely knew, could she? She was tempted but let the feeling pass. Even if Reggie wasn't part of the plot, anyone could be watching, overhearing, reporting back. She knew she was being paranoid, but it was justified, right? Besides, if she was going to talk to a stranger, she may as well go to the police. "No, I'm good." She took a step toward the courtroom. "See you back in here."

The rest of the afternoon was mind-numbing. The prosecutor, Rigley, called his first witness, Patricia Gillespie, a former employee of Shirley Mitchell who he'd promised, in his opening statement, had a lot of revelations about Mitchell's nefarious business practices. Rigley spent an hour asking background questions with no end in sight when Judge Hunt interrupted.

"Mr. Rigley, how much longer do you think you'll be with this witness?"

"A couple of hours at least, Judge."

"Then I'm going to go ahead and recess for the day and we'll start back up at nine a.m." He turned to the jury. "Remember you all took an oath, and you are not to talk to anyone about this case, or read or watch or listen to any news about it either. Get a good night's sleep because tomorrow will be a long day." He smacked his gavel and disappeared through the door behind the bench before the bailiff could say "all rise."

Brooke looked at her watch. It was only four o'clock. She should go in to work, but if she hurried, she could catch Ben home from school before he ran off to hang out with his friends. She'd done everything the voice on the phone had told her to do, but the only way she was going to be certain Ben was safe was to lay eyes on him herself. Decision made, she grabbed her purse from the jury room and headed to the parking garage. As she was driving away, she spotted Reggie walking up to a Jeep Wrangler. Reggie waved and she waved back—it was what people did, she told herself and besides, acting so standoffish was attracting more attention than being civil. The idea that Reggie was the one spying on her didn't jive with the comfort she felt when she was around her. But if someone were spying on her, that's what they'd want her to feel, right?

She pulled out of the garage and drove home. The real question was what did the mysterious stranger want from her besides serving on Shirley Mitchell's jury? Was she supposed to guarantee an outcome and, if so, how? She was one person out of twelve. She'd have one vote when the case was over. Sure, one vote could hang a jury, but she'd seen enough legal dramas on TV to know that the case could be retried if they didn't reach a verdict.

Counting on you to weigh things down.

The last message was too cryptic for her way too tired brain to figure out and she shoved it to the back of her mind. She was home within twenty minutes of leaving the courthouse and she came in to find Ben sitting at the kitchen table, shoving one of the donuts from this morning in his mouth.

"I see how it is," she said. "You wait until I'm not home and then you eat all the good stuff."

"Hey, Mom. I'm celebrating because I made a hundred on my calculus test." He waved a glazed donut at her. "This is the last good one. You want it?"

"Look at you, being all generous. It does look good, but I think I'll pass." She started to say she didn't have anything to celebrate, but decided not to burst his bubble. He deserved to bask in the glow of his good grades. She dug in her purse for the gift card she'd been saving for a special occasion and produced it with a flourish. "I was thinking we could spring for Shake Shack tonight."

"Delivery or in person?"

"Your choice."

"In person. Every time we get delivery, their fries show up cold and the shakes show up warm."

She shook her keys. "In person it is. Grab your stuff and let's go."

Ben practically ran to the car and spent the entire ride recounting how his math teacher had talked to him about joining mathletes.

She had a *Mean Girls* flashback. "Isn't that a high school thing?"

"It is, but since I'm taking AP classes, I can try out for the team and travel with them to meets if I make the cut. Mr. Lawrence said I have a good chance. Tryouts are in two weeks."

"Travel?" She tried not to instill the question with fret, but she could hear the edge in her voice, and she was certain he could too. "Like how often and where to?"

"Like to other schools who compete. The farthest school is Waco and that's only once a season. We go on a school bus and Mr. Lawrence travels with us." He bounced in his seat. "No overnights."

She took a deep breath while she contemplated how to respond without killing his enthusiasm. "Sounds pretty awesome, kiddo. Let me give it some thought."

"You have to sign a permission slip before I can try out. It's online and I sent you the link."

"I'll take a look at it."

"That sounds like a 'maybe' and 'maybe' usually means no."

"Not always."

"Mostly."

She started to deny it, but after taking a moment to reflect, she realized he was right. She often delayed her answers, not because she wanted to deny him the things he wanted, but because she wasn't always sure about the best way to keep him safe as if that were the only rubric she could use to make her decision. A few school-sponsored bus trips out of town shouldn't be an issue and normally it wouldn't be, but after the threat she'd received, she couldn't commit to the risk and she couldn't tell him why. For now, all she could do was delay and pacify him with burgers and shakes. "I promise I'll check out the link this week. Okay?"

"Yeah, okay."

She pulled up in front of Shake Shack and filed away his disappointment as another reason this week sucked beyond belief. Her rent was late, her job was in jeopardy, she was missing valuable study time, and she was getting ominous, daily threats that were so vague she wasn't sure how to comply with the demands. All she did know was that she was stuck on this jury and there was nothing she could do about it, so a double Shack burger and the largest shake on the menu were definitely in order.

CHAPTER FIVE

Reggie stood up from the workout bench and flexed her arm. "Thanks for meeting me so early."

"No worries. I'm an early bird anyway. It's when I get my best workout in."

She shook her trainer's hand and walked to the locker room. The ortho had cautioned her against pushing her recovery, but she was determined to get back to full strength as soon as possible so she could complete her firearm qualification. She likely wouldn't need a gun for the types of cases she was going to handle, and she'd never really cared for them. The shooting had only reinforced her ambivalence, but now that she'd been on the receiving end of one, she was determined to have the skills to defend herself because if it came down to her and a gunman again, she wasn't going to be the one who wound up in the hospital.

After a quick shower, she made the drive to the courthouse. The parking garage was already almost full and she had to circle several times before she found some empty spots toward the roof of the building. She pulled in at the same time as an older Subaru wagon and she glanced over to see Brooke behind the wheel—a bright spot in what promised to be a long, boring day of testimony. She took her time getting out of the car, stalling so she could walk with Brooke to the courthouse, but after a few minutes of waiting, she walked over to the driver's side window and rapped gently on the glass. When Brooke lowered the window, she leaned in. "Everything okay?"

Brooke looked flustered. "My son forgot his calculus textbook. He's going to freak out."

"Can you call him?"

"I tried and it went straight to voice mail."

"I bet he'll text you when he figures out."

"I guess so."

Reggie shrugged. "I bet someone at school has one he can use."

"It's important."

The emphatic tone in Brooke's voice signaled the forgotten text was about more than math. "I know I keep asking you this, but is everything okay?"

Brooke stared at her for a moment before her expression settled into what Reggie was certain was a fake smile. "Sure. It's all good. I'm sure I'm overreacting."

"Maybe you're not." Reggie looked at her phone. "But there's not a lot you can do about it right now. Judge Hunt is a stickler for punctuality, so we better get going." She stood back to allow Brooke space to get out of the car. "I like your ride. These babies never wear out, do they?"

"No, thank God. I don't know what I'd do if I had to add getting a new car to my to-do list."

Reggie took the opening and ran. "I guess you have a lot on your plate."

Brooke shot her a cautious look. "What's that supposed to mean?"

Uh-oh. "Well, yesterday, in court, you said you work full time and carry a full load at school. And you have a teenager." She gave a low whistle. "Sounds like a lot to me." She stopped in front of the elevator on the other side of security. "This one is tucked away from public view so it's an exception to the elevator rule."

"Twelve."

"What?" Reggie was confused at the non sequitur.

"My son is twelve. Not a teenager."

Reggie nodded, taking note of the forceful tone. "Got it. You have a twelve-year-old son who's taking Calculus. I'm thinking that sounds like even more of a handful than I originally thought."

Brooke stared at her for a moment and then laughed. "You know, you're exactly right about that."

The elevator doors opened to reveal several passengers already on board. They stepped in, but didn't continue their conversation and Reggie instantly felt the loss and wished she'd chosen the stairs instead. When they stepped out onto their floor, they walked to the courtroom in silence, as if neither one of them knew how to rethread the strings of their discussion.

Leroy was standing at the door of the jury room and when they passed by, he whispered to her, "You know better than to be late. Judge is already on the bench."

"Sorry," she whispered back. She wasn't really, considering the delay had allowed her to find out more about Brooke. She told herself her curiosity about this woman was professional practice, but she knew it was more than that. Brooke was more than a study of human behavior, she was a troubled woman.

It's none of your business.

It wasn't, but she wanted to know more and, if telling herself it was practice for being a good PI made it easier to justify poking around, then she was good with that.

She filed into the courtroom with the other jurors, disappointed that Brooke was sandwiched between Jenny and Lisa while she was stuck on the back row. Resigned to the fact she'd have to wait until lunch to talk to Brooke again, she settled in to hear more boring testimony from Patricia Gillespie. Two minutes in, her expectations were shattered.

"Tell the jury why you went to the police about your boss, Shirley Mitchell." Johnny Rigley fired off the command and leaned back in his chair.

"Because she threatened to harm my family."

Johnny abruptly stood up and started walking toward the witness stand. He cupped a hand to his ear. "I'm sorry, can you repeat that?"

"Shirley Mitchell said she would harm my family if I didn't do what she asked or if I reported her business practices."

Johnny turned toward the jury and slowly surveyed their faces. Reggie had seen this maneuver before from just about every lawyer at the courthouse and recognized the theater for what it was. The silent emphasis on the witness's words was definitely effective. Every juror in the box was riveted on Patricia, and eager to hear more.

Except for Brooke. It was almost imperceptible, but she was squirming in her chair and her gaze was not on Johnny or Patricia. For a brief second, their eyes locked and Reggie raised her eyebrows in question, but Brooke's only response was to look away. Reggie filed the event away for further inspection, but in the meantime, she turned her attention back to the front of the room, waiting for Patricia's next words.

"What exactly did Ms. Mitchell say to you?"

"I'm not sure you want me to repeat the exact words." Patricia looked up at Judge Hunt.

"Actually, I do," Rigley said. "I'm sure the judge has heard just about everything in this room. The most important thing is for you to be as accurate as you can about what you remember."

Leland rose to her feet. "Objection, Your Honor. Mr. Rigley is spending way too much time building up momentum for testimony that is going nowhere fast. If the witness has something to say, can she simply say it without all the theatrics?"

Speaking of theatrics. Reggie resisted an eye roll.

"Ms. Gillespie, please simply answer Mr. Rigley's question."

She scooted to the edge of her seat and leaned into the microphone. "She said that if I didn't like the way she got things done, I didn't have to…" She paused and took a deep breath. "*Fucking* work for her, but to consider my decision carefully if I cared about the well-being of my family."

Rigley had winced slightly at the profanity but seemed to recover quickly. "And you took that to a be a threat?"

"Wouldn't you?"

Rigley frowned, presumably at the way his own witness barked at him, but he quickly segued into another question. "Did anything happen to make you think there was a serious threat against your family?"

"Yes. A couple of days after her threat, my daughter came home from school and when she emptied her backpack, she found a note inside."

Rigley nodded and walked back to the prosecution table. He lifted a plastic sleeve from the surface and carried it back over to Patricia. "Is this the note?"

Patricia stared at it for a moment and nodded.

"You have to answer out loud," Rigley said.

"Yes, that's the note."

"Can you read it for the jury?"

She took a deep breath and there was a long pause before she launched in. "Tell your mother to do the right thing if she wants you to be able to finish school." She pointed at the note. "I realize it doesn't sound threatening out loud, but," she held the note up toward the jury, "it's written in letters cut from a magazine. I mean who does that other than a serial killer?"

Several members of the jury gasped, and Brooke's face went ashen. Gloria Leland shot to her feet. "Objection."

Judge Hunt sighed. "Strike that last part as unresponsive."

Rigley turned to the jury and raised his shoulders as if to say, "you all know the truth, right?" He leaned in. "Did anything happen after you received the note?"

"Yes. I started getting phone calls late at night. The voice on the other end of the phone was fake, you know, like they were talking through one of those things that distorts your voice."

Reggie heard a tiny squeak and looked down at Brooke who was covering her mouth with her hand. This testimony was provoking some very personal reactions from Brooke, and she was determined to find out why, but right now all she could do was sit tight and listen. Patricia was a compelling witness, but Reggie wasn't quite convinced she wasn't stretching it with the accusation that a high-profile developer like Shirley Mitchell would resort to threatening notes and phone calls. All she'd really have had to do to ruin Patricia was pick up the phone and blackball her to every other employer in town. But if the threats were real and Shirley wasn't behind them, then who was?

❖

Out of the corner of her eye, Brooke spotted Reggie walking toward her. She looked around and homed in on one of the younger male jurors who was standing by himself across the room. He'd worn a tie each day and he seemed a little dorky which made her think of Ben. She walked briskly toward him, certain Reggie was following her and determined not to look back.

"Hi," she said, sticking her hands out. "I'm Brooke. What's your name?"

"Mark."

Not super talkative, apparently. She smiled big, hopefully not so big she'd scare him, and tried another tack. "I'm usually okay with names, but after hearing all the names yesterday, I got jumbled. How do you feel about being on the jury?"

He frowned like it was a weird question. Maybe it was, but it was open-ended enough to get more than a one-word answer.

"I guess it's okay. Kind of boring."

She nodded. "Not the most exciting case. I mean, don't get me wrong, it's good no one died or was injured, but rich people arguing about money—not exactly riveting."

"We're not supposed to be talking about the case."

Brooke turned to find Reggie standing to her left. Close. Really close. "We're not talking about the case," she said, spotting Mark ease away out of the corner of her eye. Great. Now she was going to be known as the busybody, troublemaker. "We were talking about being bored."

"And that's different because?"

"Because we weren't discussing the evidence, only the presentation."

"Again, I don't see the difference."

She couldn't tell if Reggie was being obtuse or just enjoyed messing with her. Either way, she wanted out of this conversation. "That's cool. You do you." She started to back away and bumped into Lisa and noticed the other jurors had started to crowd around them.

"Are you talking about the case?" Lisa asked.

"No!" Brooke said, perhaps a little too emphatically. Suddenly she'd become the center of attention and she needed to escape.

"I think it's okay for us to talk about what we've seen so far as long as we don't make any decisions," Jenny said.

"It's not, actually," Reggie said. "The instructions were pretty clear."

"They must not have been that clear or we wouldn't all have different opinions about it," Jenny said in a snarky tone. "Right, Brooke?"

Shit. She held up her hands in surrender. "I could be wrong. I mean, I'm not the one who works here."

"That's right," one of the other men, Jack something, said, pointing at Reggie. "You work at the courthouse. What did you do here?"

Reggie frowned. "I don't work here. I used to."

"That's right, you were shot when that crazy guy opened fire in the courtroom. Didn't you work for one of the judges?"

The frown twisted deeper, and Reggie backed up. "I don't work here anymore, but I do know Judge Hunt said not to discuss the case and I know for a fact he meant any aspect of it."

Brooke wanted to argue the point. It was obvious Reggie was taking the judge's instructions too literally and she didn't appreciate being schooled in front of the rest of the jury. She'd said cases about money were boring and more so than cases about people getting physically hurt and she stood by that. And arguing with Reggie would only draw attention to herself—one of the things she wasn't supposed to do, so instead of trying to get the last word, she ducked out the door and went to the restroom, taking a few extra minutes to clear her head. It worked until she walked out the door to find Reggie standing a foot away.

"You have to stop doing that."

"What?" Reggie asked.

"Following me everywhere. I'm beginning to think you're spying on me." She floated the words and watched closely for Reggie's reaction.

"I'm not."

"So, you're out here waiting to go into the bathroom?"

Reggie kicked a toe at the carpet. "Uh, well, not really."

Brooke stared at her for a moment. She detected no signs of deception. Either Reggie was really good at spying on her or she was completely innocent. Either way she wanted to know and impulse pushed her to say, "Next time you want to give me a note, don't leave it in my bag. That's creepy." She watched for Reggie's reaction, but at first there was nothing but a blank stare. No flicker of recognition, no nod, nothing. Several more seconds passed, and Reggie finally spoke.

"Okay."

She turned and walked back into the jury room, and Brooke watched her go wondering what had just happened and whether she'd made a horrible mistake.

She waited until Reggie was completely out of sight, and pulled out her phone. She fired off a text.

Asserting mom privilege. Ping me back to say you're okay.

She hit send and waited. One minute. Two. If he was in class, he couldn't text. Other kids would do it anyway, but not Ben. She needed to introduce a mom exception to the no texting in school rule.

She stared at the screen. She stared at the wall. She stared back at the screen. She could hear the rest of the jury stirring behind the wall of the juror room. It was almost time to go back into the courtroom and after being late this morning, she didn't want to be the one who held things up this afternoon. Especially not after the scene just now. Dammit, Ben. Answer your damn phone.

All good.

The two words brought huge relief and she breathed deep. Whatever had happened in calculus, Ben had survived it, but she'd been worried about way more than that. All was well. For now. She vowed to keep her mouth shut and head down for the rest of this trial. Let know-it-alls like Reggie Knoll be the center of attention.

When they all walked back into the courtroom, Jenny and Lisa flanked her and shot Reggie disdainful looks in a show of solidarity. She barely knew these women and she wasn't sure she liked them, but the weird dynamics of being trapped in a small group and sequestered from information bound them together. Rule number two played through her head: don't mingle or talk to the other jurors. Well, that ship had sailed through no fault of her own. Nothing she could do now but embrace the fact she wasn't entirely alone.

Rigley passed the witness shortly after the break and Gloria Leland leaned way back in her seat with her arms crossed in front of her chest for an uncomfortably long time without asking any questions.

"Do you have any cross-examination for this witness?" Judge Hunt finally asked.

Gloria sighed and pushed off from the table. "My apologies, Judge. I'm not entirely sure where to begin." She took a moment to sift through the papers in front of her, ultimately setting them to the side with a small huff. She stared at Patricia long enough to have her squirming in her chair before she asked her first question and when she did, it caught her totally off guard.

"How's your family?"

A puzzled expression crossed Patricia's face before she schooled her features back into the somber look she'd worn throughout her testimony. "I'm sorry, what?"

Gloria turned toward the jury and raised her eyebrows like she was inviting them into her mental space. "You testified that my client threatened your family, right?"

"True."

"She threatened to hurt them."

"Yes."

"If you reported her." Gloria flicked another glance at the jury before boring her eyes into Patricia's until she was certain

Patricia knew exactly where she was going with her questions. "Right?"

"Yes, but once I reported her to the police she knew she'd get in trouble if she tried anything."

"That's interesting. So, what you're saying is Ms. Mitchell wouldn't do anything if she thought law enforcement might take action against her?"

"Exactly."

Gloria smiled brightly. "Isn't that how laws work? I mean, I like to drive ninety miles an hour on the tollway, but fear of getting pulled over keeps me in the seventy range." She waited a beat, but Patricia was still scrambling for a response. "Never mind, let's pretend that was a rhetorical question. But I have another one for you."

Patricia looked like she wanted to crawl under the seat while she waited for the next round. Gloria slowly walked back to counsel table and opened a folder. She skimmed the contents, closed it, and stuck it in the crook of her arm. "How much was your bonus for last year?"

Patricia looked confused at the complete change of subject. "I'm not entirely sure."

"Fine, let's try this another way. Was it more or less than the year before?"

"I'm not sure I recall."

"Are you sure about that?" She drummed her fingers on the edge of the folder.

"It might have been lower than the previous year."

"It was thirty percent lower." She held up the folder. "Would you like to see the paperwork?" Patricia shook her head. "Do you think that was because you went tattling to law enforcement?"

Patricia stared at Gloria for a moment like she was trying to assess if she was laying a trap. "No, because the bonus structure was set up before I talked to her about my concerns."

Again with the smile. "That's right," Gloria said. "I appreciate you pointing that out." She walked back to the table and tossed the folder down. She pulled out her chair and started to sit down but before her butt was in the seat, she stood back up and held up a finger. "I thought of one more thing."

The entire courtroom went silent, and the air was thick with tension before she finally spoke. "Is it possible you threatened to turn in your employer because you were unhappy with your bonus?"

Patricia's face reddened, whether it was from anger or guilt was hard to tell, and when she opened her mouth to answer, Brooke was sure a tirade was coming, but Gloria beat her to the punch. "Never mind. That was another one of those rhetorical questions. Everyone wants to hear the answer, but no one believes it."

"How dare you imply I would tell a lie because I was unhappy about money."

"No further questions, Your Honor." Gloria sat down and stared at Patricia, her calm expression serving as an agitating force threatening to send Patricia spiraling out of control. Rigley asked a few follow-up questions to try to blunt the edge of Gloria's remarks, but the damage had been done. When Brooke walked out of the courtroom at the end of the day, she couldn't help but think she knew a little bit of how Patricia was feeling.

CHAPTER SIX

Reggie waited at the courthouse to give Brooke time to get to her car and exit the garage. She had no idea what Brooke's accusation about a note and her purse meant, but she figured Brooke didn't want to see her and she was too tired after the long day to argue anymore.

"Hey, Reggie. What're you doing here? I heard you were going to work in the free world."

She looked up to see Marty Lafferty, the bailiff from her old court. He'd gotten it worse than she had in the shooting, and she was surprised to see him here. "The question is what are *you* doing here?"

He held up a badge and grinned. "Doing the paperwork to start back at my old job. Almost. I'll be in Judge Aguilar's courtroom. First day is Monday next."

She shook her head. Marty had been covering for another bailiff the day of the shooting when he dived in front of Judge Aguilar to keep her from getting shot, taking several bullets in the process. He was a goddammed hero and deserved to never have to work again, let alone at the place where he'd almost lost his life. "I can't believe you're coming back here."

"What else am I going to do?" He asked. "This is the only life I've ever known. I'm two years away from full retirement.

You think I'm going to give that up for some punk who's not even a good shot?"

"You're a good person, Marty." Her gut roiled at the idea of coming back to work here. "Better than me."

"Nah, just doing the only thing I know how to do. Not like anyone else is going to hire an old geezer like me." He clasped her good shoulder. "You've got your whole life ahead of you. No reason for you to relive what happened every day when you get out of here and do anything you want."

"I guess so." Most of the people who worked at the courthouse considered it a calling and she had too. Before the shooting. But the bullet through her arm had changed her perspective. She'd floundered for a while, unsure what she wanted to do before she settled on the legal-adjacent career of private investigator. Lennox's friend, Skye Keaton, one of the well-known PIs in the community, had promised to show her the ropes and feed her some leads, and she'd finally managed to wrap her mind around the new route her life was taking, but running into Marty brought guilt bubbling up inside. "It's hard being back here for a lot of reasons, but there's a part of me that will always wonder if I should've given it another chance."

"You don't owe anyone anything," Marty said. "Try something new and if you ever decide you want to come back, I'm sure your people will find a place for you." He paused for a moment. "The only other advice I have to give is don't lose contact with your people. You may decide you never want to work here again, but don't throw away the friendships you've made because the career isn't for you. These people are what got me back on my feet. I don't know what I'd do without them."

His words pierced the veneer she'd struggled to keep in place and tears started to form. The thing she missed the most was the easy camaraderie of the people who worked here—no matter what side they were on, with only a few exceptions, they could come together at the end of the day and celebrate wins, mourn losses, and support each other with unconditional generosity. Striking out on her own meant she'd have to be her own cheering section, grief counselor, and everything else. She could do it, but it wouldn't be easy.

She was still deep in thought about the consequences of her career move when she walked into the parking garage a few minutes later, and it took a moment to register the angry tone of the whispered conversation that was happening near her car. When she recognized Brooke's voice, she ducked behind a column, still determined not to run into her again today.

Only snippets of conversation were audible: "threatening," "cryptic," "unjustly accused." She strained to hear more, but the voices got lower as the exchange progressed.

When the conversation abruptly ended, Reggie poked her head out from behind the column to try to get a glimpse at whoever'd been involved in the heated exchange with Brooke, but all she saw was Brooke standing beside her car. She had a choice to make. She could walk over to her car and pretend like she'd heard nothing, or she could ask her what was going on. Marty's words echoed in her head—about the camaraderie at the courthouse, the way people came together no matter what side they were on. She might not have been able to hear the conversation, but she could tell by the expression on Brooke's face it had upset her and she was compelled to address it head-on.

Choice made, she stepped out from behind the column and strode over to her car. As she approached, she knew she'd made the right decision because Brooke was shaking. She sped up until she was standing close. "Hey, what happened?"

"What are you doing here?"

Reggie pointed to her car. "Nothing shady, I promise. Just figured I'd leave like everyone else." She waited a beat. "I couldn't help but hear you talking to that guy. Was he threatening you?"

"Why would you say that?"

Reggie took note Brooke wasn't denying the threat. "Because you look shaken up and it sounded like the conversation got a little heated."

Brooke sagged against her car. "If I said I don't want to talk about it, would you respect that?"

"Of course," Reggie replied. "But if you did want to talk about it, I'd be happy to listen. Look, you don't know me, but up until a few months ago, I was a court coordinator here. I worked directly for one of the judges and my job was to manage her docket which included working with defendants, witnesses, victims, and attorneys on both sides of a case. Not trying to brag, but I've got mad listening skills and there's pretty much nothing I haven't heard."

"I thought we weren't supposed to talk outside of the courtroom."

Reggie heard the wistful tone in Brooke's voice and suspected she really did want to talk, but something was holding her back. "We're not supposed to talk about the case, but that doesn't mean we can't talk about other stuff."

"If someone's watching, how will they know the difference?"

Reggie glanced around, but they were the only ones on this floor of the garage. Brooke was probably concerned the guy she'd been talking to earlier was still around and maybe he was. She leaned in close. "Who was the guy?"

Brooke flinched slightly, but she whispered back. "Please don't ask."

"I won't, but I need something in exchange."

Brooke's eyes narrowed. "What?"

"Ice cream. I've been craving it all day. I have a lot of work to do tonight and I'm afraid if I don't satisfy my craving, I'll never be able to focus." Reggie held up her keys and jingled them in the air. "You game?" She watched several different expressions play across Brooke's face and braced for a no, but when Brooke finally answered she was pleasantly surprised.

"Okay, but I want to pick the place."

❖

Brooke looked in the rearview mirror again, not sure why she was surprised to see Reggie still following her. She told herself she'd only agreed to ice cream so she could bring some home to Ben, but the truth was she needed the comfort and company of another adult even if she wouldn't be able to share the details of what was plaguing her.

While she drove, she replayed the conversation with the stranger who'd been waiting at her car.

"I've done what you've asked me to do. Why are you still threatening me?"

"It's not a threat. It's a promise. It's time for you to take the next step."

"Then tell me what it is and stop being so damn cryptic."

"The woman on trial has been unjustly accused. It's up to you to make it right."

"Still cryptic. I'm one person out of twelve. There's nothing I can do."

"You have two choices. You either convince the rest to vote with you or you hold out no matter what. I suggest you start laying the groundwork tomorrow."

"And if I don't?"

"You know the risk and what's important to you. If you want to avoid the harm, you'll do what's asked of you."

"Who are you?"

"A concerned citizen. You know what to do."

He'd left abruptly after his "concerned citizen" pronouncement, and she hadn't had time to process the interaction before Reggie appeared out of nowhere. The timing was suspicious, but it was possible she was reading too much into it since Reggie had parked next to her and they'd all been dismissed from court at the same time. Didn't matter. As much as she might want to, confiding in Reggie could spell disaster and it wasn't a chance she was willing to take. Not when Ben's life could be at stake.

But a quick trip for ice cream was an innocuous venture and it might make her feel a little more normal. She pulled into the parking lot at Braum's and found a space near the front door. She didn't wait for Reggie to park, but she stood outside the front door until she appeared beside her.

"Braum's. Interesting choice."

Brooke stiffened slightly. "Look, I know there are a ton of fancy new places with funky new flavors, but this is my favorite and it's my son's favorite, and I'll fight anyone who thinks it's not as good as the others."

Reggie raised her hands in the air. "No need to fight. I completely agree. It's old school, but it's one of the best." She opened the door. "After you?"

Brooke led the way and ordered a cone with cherries, pecans, and cream and Reggie ordered one with rocky road. Reggie insisted on paying and she didn't have the energy to argue. They sat down at a booth and enjoyed their ice cream in silence, and for a few minutes Brooke managed to shut out everything else: her precarious employment, whether she'd passed her Econ exam, the fact she was stuck on jury duty, and the threat on her son's life that hung on her complying with the whim of a stranger she didn't even understand.

"What's your son's name?"

And there went her relaxation. She hesitated for a moment before deciding the question wasn't too personal and she'd look like a weirdo for refusing to answer. "Ben."

"And you said he's twelve?"

She had to admit she was impressed Reggie remembered. "Twelve going on forty."

Reggie smiled. "I get that. Smart kid?"

"Genius level. But a little socially awkward so while he can ace any test put in front of him, a school dance will have him spinning out."

"Does he get that from you or his dad?"

She stared into Reggie's eyes for a minute, trying to read intent. It was probably an innocent question, but it didn't feel that way. Of course, nothing felt right since she'd first received the call about the jury summons, which prompted her to ask. "When did you get your jury summons?"

Reggie looked surprised by the question. "Last month. Why?"

Brooke shook her head. "No reason." She wondered if anyone else on the jury had just received their summons. If throwing the case was so important to the mysterious stranger, it seems like they would've wanted to ensure their fate wasn't entirely in one juror's hands. Then again, they'd be stupid to pick Reggie since she had courthouse connections. "How's your ice cream?" she asked, to change the subject.

"It's good, but I get the impression you want to talk about something else."

Brooke took another bite to avoid having to answer. She wanted to confide in someone, and Reggie seemed as good a person as any, but she imagined how things would go. She'd tell Reggie she'd been threatened and Reggie would insist they inform Judge Hunt. Judge Hunt would insist on questioning her and she'd refuse to answer. She wasn't sure what would happen next, but she suspected it wouldn't be good.

"What happens if we can't reach a verdict?"

"For someone who didn't want to discuss the case, you sure do have a lot of questions about the process."

Brooke shrugged, feigning nonchalance. "It's new to me. I like to know what to expect."

"If we don't reach a verdict, he can make us stick around until we do, and if that doesn't work, he can declare a hung jury. The prosecutor can try the case again if they want to, but in the meantime, there's no conviction. Mitchell's not in jail, but if she was there would be a hearing to determine if she should remain there pending the new trial."

"Do you think the prosecutor would try the case again?"

"Hell yeah. It's a high-profile trial and they've already made a big deal out of it in the local press. Rigley and the entire DA's office would look silly if they decided not to move forward."

Brooke licked her ice cream and contemplated the scenario. If she hung the jury, there'd be a new one. Would the person threatening her find a new potential jury to intimidate into voting his way? Would they keep doing that until they managed to pull off a "not guilty"? Did that even make sense? Or were they stalling, hoping something else happened with the case before an unfavorable verdict came down? Either way she was stuck in the middle for now and there was no sense talking about it so she changed the subject. "Did you grow up in Dallas?"

"I did. Lived here my whole life. My folks moved to Plano a few years ago, but I live in a condo near downtown. Makes it easy to get to the courthouse in the morning."

"Do you miss working there?"

"Sometimes yes, sometimes no." Reggie started off into the distance. "I miss the people. It's hard to be around a group of people for hours a day, many days of the week, and then suddenly not have them in your life anymore."

"I can see that. Are there good people at your new job?"

"There are no people at my new job." Reggie cracked a half smile. "I'm studying to take the licensing exam so I can be a private investigator and once I pass the test, I'll be in business solo."

"That's a big change, right?"

"Huge. I think I'm ready for it, but…"

"But?"

"But it is harder than I thought it would be not to have pals on board."

Brooke heard the wistfulness in Reggie's voice. "Hey, you could be really successful and wind up having to hire new people really soon."

Reggie met her eyes. "Good point. I'll hope for that." She crunched the last bite of her cone. "What do you do for a living?"

"I started back to school to get the bachelor's degree I abandoned when I got pregnant with Ben, and I'm working at Dante's to pay tuition and bills. It's not ideal, but it won't last forever. I have to say jury duty really cuts into the bill paying part of the equation."

"That's a big load. I'm guessing Ben's dad is not in the equation?"

"He hasn't been for a very long time. I don't even know where he is."

"I bet if you'd explained your situation to Judge Hunt, he would've excused you from serving."

"I didn't even think of that." Brooke smiled to cover the lie. "But it might not have worked anyway. Remember, you didn't think you'd get picked."

"Word. Not sure what happened there."

"Maybe they thought you'd be extra fair since you've worked at the courthouse."

"More like someone wasn't thinking at all."

The conversation trailed off and they sat in silence for a bit. Brooke wasn't sure what else to say that didn't involve tiptoeing around the subject of the case, but she was fairly confident Reggie wasn't involved with whoever had been threatening her and that was something. She crunched the last bit of her cone and crushed her napkin into a tiny ball.

"Ready to go?" Reggie asked.

"Yes, but I need a pint of rocky road for the kid."

Reggie was out of her seat in a flash, headed for the dairy section. She grabbed a quart of rocky road and was headed to the cash register when Brooke intercepted her. "What are you doing?"

"Contributing to the cause." Reggie pulled out a twenty and handed it to the clerk.

"I can buy my own ice cream."

"I have no doubt you can, but I'd like to do this for you. Consider it a peace offering."

She should say no and insist on paying. She wasn't so destitute she couldn't afford to buy ice cream for her son. But Reggie was trying to be nice, and after their disagreement earlier, accepting her gesture of goodwill was an easy thing to do. "Fine, but next time the ice cream's on me."

"Fair enough." Reggie took the bag from the cashier and handed it to her. "I'm going to take off since I still have a lot of studying to do. See you tomorrow. Have a good night."

Brooke stood in the middle of Braum's and watched her go. She'd been certain she wanted to be alone with her thoughts, but after spending a short time with Reggie, she wasn't sure being alone was the answer for any of her problems. She desperately wanted to tell someone about her situation, but as long as Ben was in danger, she couldn't, but if she could tell someone Reggie would be the one. Too trusting? Perhaps, but it wasn't like she was going to act on the instinct. If she could only get through this trial, then maybe there'd be room in life for friendships with people like Reggie. Or even something more.

CHAPTER SEVEN

"Mom, are you still in bed?"

Brooke's eyes shot open and she scrambled to sit up. The sheets were twisted, her pillow was on the floor, and the textbook for her marketing class was lying open on the comforter, pages crinkled around the edges. Yes. Yes, she was still in bed and apparently, she'd fallen asleep while studying for her next exam. She flipped her phone over and stared at the time. Eight a.m.

Shit. Shit. Shit. Ben was late, she was late, and she was totally screwed. "I'm up. I'm up. Be right out! Meet you in the kitchen."

She knew that he knew she was lying, but she didn't have time to worry about it. If things were normal, she'd stick him in the back of an Uber so at least he'd be on time, but recent stranger danger kept her from taking that route.

She jumped in the shower, rinsed off, and stood in front of the mirror, glad she had long hair since it gave her options. She tossed in a messy up-do, threw on some powder and blush, and shimmied into pants and a sweater, hoping they matched. She slipped on loafers, grabbed her purse, and dashed into the kitchen, but Ben wasn't there. After calling out his name several times, she searched the apartment, but he was nowhere in sight.

Her phone pinged to signal a text. *Got a ride with Mia from Calc. See you later.*

Mia from Calc? She racked her brain for a memory of him mentioning any girl, let alone one named Mia, before, but couldn't come up with an instance. His calculus class was at the local high school which meant Mia was at least two years older, maybe more. She clicked on his number and waited impatiently through the rings.

"Hi, Mom. It's all good. I'm with Mia."

She was certain she heard an echo on the line. "Am I on speaker, Ben?"

The echo instantly disappeared. "Not anymore."

"Who's Mia?"

"She's a sophomore in my Calc class. Very smart. She's in mathletes."

"And she just happened to be around to take you to school today?" Brooke knew she probably sounded ridiculous, but she pushed on. "I told you I'd take you."

"You have to get to the courthouse. I get it. Mia and I were texting about the assignment anyway and she offered."

"Where are you?"

"We're pulling up to the school right now."

"Text me Mia's last name and number so I have it in my phone. And tell her I said thanks. Text me when you get inside. Love you."

"Love you too, Mom," he said with only a hint of a sigh.

She waited for his text, saved Mia's number in her phone, and headed to her car. Ben was fine. A fifteen-year-old sophomore wasn't going to corrupt her kid, and she was thankful he'd been resourceful enough to have a backup plan since she'd failed miserably at being a good mom this morning. The best thing she could do today was show up at the courthouse, do what she was told, and put this entire episode of her life behind her so she could focus on graduating from school, getting a good job with regular hours and benefits, and spending more quality time with Ben.

When she pushed through the door to the jury room, Leroy gave her serious side eye, but she knew for a fact she was exactly on time. She spotted Reggie standing on the other side of the room and started to walk toward her when she remembered her instructions. Don't mingle with the other jurors. She'd already blown that, but if she could get through the rest of this trial without breaking the rules, then she'd be free to talk to Reggie all she wanted. And she wanted to a lot.

"Let's go, everyone," Leroy said. "Judge Hunt wants to pack as much into today as possible, so everyone needs to keep a close eye on the time during breaks and lunch."

Brooke nearly rolled her eyes at the remark which was clearly directed at her, but she dutifully fell in line with the rest of the jurors. Reggie managed to line up right behind her and whispered in her ear.

"Don't mind him. He's all bluster. Besides, it's not like he's going to toss you off the jury for being a few minutes late."

"Like that would be a bad thing." Brooke wanted to bite back the words the minute she said them in case there was anyone in the room spying on behalf of mystery man. "Just kidding. I'm happy to serve."

Reggie gave her a puzzled look which she ignored. She knew her pendulum mood swings sounded crazy, but she was feeling pretty crazy, so it tracked. They filed into the courtroom and took their seats.

The next few hours consisted of bone-dry testimony about financial reports. The forensic expert for the prosecution gleefully described a series of debits and credits that, in his words, showed a pattern of deceit tied to hiding funds paid to public officials for several development projects, but all she heard when he spoke was a bunch of blah, blah, blahs that made her head spin. The judge skipped the morning break, and by the time they stopped for lunch, she had a massive headache. Lisa and Jenny asked if she wanted to join them in the cafeteria, but she made an excuse about needing to get some air and left the jury room on her own.

She spotted Reggie ducking into a courtroom down the hall and wondered if she was going to visit some friends from when she'd worked there. Brooke couldn't remember the last time she'd hung out with friends. Since she'd started school, she'd no free time and everyone had gotten tired of her breaking plans at the last minute on a regular basis either because she had to work, study, or be around for Ben. It wasn't like she didn't want to hang out with them, but one day, not that long from now, she was going to need to be able to pay for the kind of college Ben deserved and it wasn't going to be cheap. Couple that with being a single parent and there wasn't any free time to spend hanging out with pals.

She dug in her purse and seized on a granola bar that was likely out of date, but sustenance enough to mean she could forgo the cafeteria in favor of going outside for some fresh air. She took the stairs down to the lobby and walked out the front door, enjoying the light breeze and the warmth of the sunshine on her face. She wandered around for a bit and settled on one of the steps off to the right of the entrance—a perfect place for people watching. At this time of day, there were more people leaving than arriving and she found herself guessing whether things had gone their way by the way they walked and the expressions they wore. She'd evaluated the fifth person and was fully caught up in the game when she heard a voice to her left that caught her attention.

"Because it's Shirley freakin' Mitchell. She goes down and we'll all be right behind her. Do I really have to spell what happens next?" A moment of silence and then, "Exactly. Stick with the plan."

Brooke didn't hear anything after that, and she casually turned her head to see if she could tell who'd been talking. She spotted several people standing in various places on the steps on their phones. Two of them had their backs to her and the third was a woman. She eliminated the last since the voice she'd heard was deep and masculine and turned her attention to the others. She mentally willed the two men to turn around, but neither did and a few minutes later one of them walked toward the garage and the other into the courthouse. She considered following one, but reason stopped her. What would she do if she caught up to them? She hadn't seen the face of the man who'd accosted her in the parking garage so she wouldn't know if it was the same person, and even if she did, what would she say? "I remember how you threatened me, and I heard you on the phone just now talking about Shirley Mitchell." So what? She didn't know what the plan was the man had been referring to although she suspected the threat against her might be part of it. But there was no real proof—only her gut telling her the conversation she'd heard was important. What was she going to do about it?

❖

Harry Benton's trial was in full swing, complete with a packed gallery of spectators and press cameras crowded into the last row. Reggie's attention was drawn to the jury first, partly out of sympathy, but mostly in relief. Shirley Mitchell's was fairly high profile, but her trial wasn't as headline-grabbing as this one. These jurors were being scrutinized by all of Dallas.

She spotted Skye Keaton in one of the rows toward the back of the room and Skye waved her over, making room next to her.

"I didn't think you were going to show up," Skye whispered.

"I didn't make a special trip for it. I'm stuck in jury duty up on seven. Hunt's court."

"Shirley Mitchell's case?"

"That's the one." Reggie glanced around. "It's a pain, but not a circus like this one."

"Shirley didn't show up at a judge's house threatening to ruin her life."

"True." Reggie stared at the back of Benton's head and then at the cop on the stand. "How's it going?"

At that moment, the judge called a recess for lunch, and everyone stood while the jurors filed out of the room, but most of the spectators stayed put, likely afraid they'd lose their seats if they wandered off.

"Slow. There's been a lot of breaks and jury selection took forever. They're just now laying the foundation for what happened at Judge Aguilar's place. I'm sure once they get to hers and Franco's testimony things will start to get interesting," she said, referring to Judge Aguilar's girlfriend who'd shown up in the middle of Benton's threats on the judge.

"How did you get out of testifying?"

"Franco can handle my part. The ADAs are trying to keep it lean and mean. They feel like if they keep the evidence related to the threat on Aguilar, they're more likely to get a conviction. They can throw in other stuff during punishment or save it for another trial. The end game is to put him away forever, but if for some reason he gets off on this charge, jeopardy will not have attached to other possible charges."

Reggie knew enough about the law to recognize the strategy made sense. "How long do you think it will last?"

"I figure they'll wrap up testimony by the end of the week or early next. The real question is how long it'll take for the jury to deliberate."

"Speaking of juries, I better get back to mine." Reggie started to stand up, but Skye motioned for her to stay seated. "You give any more thought to my offer?"

She'd shoved Skye's offer to the back of her mind the moment she'd heard it. Most new PIs would jump at the chance to work for one of the top private detectives in Dallas, and since

Skye was often hired for high-profile cases and didn't have any other investigators working for her. Reggie would get to work on lots of interesting cases. But they'd all be criminal since Skye didn't take what she called silly civil disputes. She'd be back at this courthouse on a regular basis, interviewing defendants and witnesses and testifying in court. Exactly the opposite of what she wanted, which made the conversation a nonstarter.

"I can't do it."

Skye's smile was indulgent. "You can. I know from experience that if you don't get back up after a bad experience, it can keep you down for good. You think you're making a good choice for yourself by taking a new course, but you're headed in the wrong direction. You're cut out for this, not that silly stuff you've convinced yourself is harmless. It will eat your soul." She stuck out a hand. "Call me when you change your mind."

Reggie was replaying Skye's words when she walked back into the jury room in Hunt's court so lost in thought she almost ran into Brooke who was entering at the same time. She backed up so Brooke could go in first. "After you."

"Do we have to?" Brooke said.

"Unfortunately, yes." Reggie followed her into the room. "I wanted to go downstairs and get a snack, but I ran out of time. I bet a million dollars they leave us kicking around in here for another thirty minutes."

"Seems to happen a lot."

"True. What did you do with your free time?"

Brooke looked flustered at the question, and she didn't answer right away. "You don't have to tell me," Reggie said. "I was just making conversation. I went and checked in on another trial that's going on here this week."

"And here I thought you didn't want to be at the courthouse anymore. Can't get enough?"

"That one's personal."

Brooke's eyes widened. "Is it the guy who shot you?"

"The guy who hired the guy who shot me and several others—Harry Benton. His trial isn't about that, but it may be the only satisfaction any of his victims get. The DA is prosecuting him for threatening a judge—the woman I was talking to in the cafeteria the other day. It's kind of confusing and I'm not sure I really get the strategy, but I don't have a say in it."

"That sounds frustrating."

"I try not to think about it too much."

"Yet, you looked in on the trial. How's that going?"

"About as riveting as this one."

Brooke reached for her hand and squeezed it. "I hope the guy goes away for a very long time."

Reggie had barely warmed to the touch when Brooke let go. The movement had happened so quickly, she would've thought she'd imagined it, but the effect of her touch lingered. Protective, sweet, thoughtful. She'd needed the connection more than she realized. "Thank you."

The rest of the day went surprisingly fast. Rigley called a succession of witnesses whose testimony was quick and to the point. The theme was simple: Mitchell had a history of seeking favors from local officials, and often skirted close to the line between influence and bribery. Gloria punched back at each of the prosecution witnesses in an attempt to imply that her client had engaged in the same kind of behavior anyone with business was expected to if they wanted to get anything done. The back and forth went on the rest of the day, and when the judge finally recessed for the day, Reggie could hardly believe it was already five o'clock.

She ran into Brooke again as they were leaving the jury room, and they walked to the garage together. They were almost there when she mustered the courage to say, "I don't suppose you'd like to go for ice cream again."

"Twice in one week?"

"Yeah, I know. It's a long shot. Besides, you don't look like the kind of woman who indulges on that level." She didn't even try to hide the fact she was flirting.

"You'd be surprised."

Was Brooke flirting back with her or was she so out of the game, she didn't know the difference? "So, you're in?"

"I can't," Brooke said, looking genuinely disappointed. "I promised my son I'd help him with a project. Not that I understand half of what he's studying. But I do make a mean flash card."

"I'm sure you do more than that."

"Lots of moral support if that counts for anything."

Reggie flashed back to her conversation with Skye. "It does. Trust me, it does."

Brooke pointed to her car. "Guess I better go." She lingered for a moment before she opened the door like she wanted to say something more, but after a moment of silence she waved and said, "See you tomorrow."

Reggie kept walking and resisted looking back. Brooke had a lot going on and so did she. The bubble of jury duty might make it seem otherwise, but she had no business trying to start something with anyone while she should be studying for her exam and starting her new career, let alone a woman with a young son, a full-time job, and a college degree in the balance. Flirty ice cream dates be damned.

She got into her Jeep and was driving out of the garage when she spotted Brooke's car still parked with Brooke behind the wheel looking like she was about to cry. Without thinking, she pulled over into a space nearby, walked over, and rapped on the window. Brooke cracked the door.

"Is everything okay?"

"He won't start."

"He?"

"The car's name is Seth. We've known each other a very long time."

"He seems to have served you well. Do you have AAA?"

"I barely have enough money to pay to get out of this parking garage, so no. And before you ask, I've done all the usual things. I know his quirks, and this is something new."

"Okay." Reggie suppressed the urge to ask her specifics. Brooke clearly knew her own car better than anyone else and would be insulted if she acted like she was the expert here. "What would you like to do?"

"I guess I better get an Uber home."

"I know something cheaper than an Uber." She pointed to her Jeep. "How about I give you a ride and we can figure out your car tomorrow. I bet Leroy has some extra parking vouchers sitting around that he can give you to keep you from racking up a big bill." She watched Brooke glance furtively around as she struggled with whether to accept her offer.

"Thank you."

"Not a problem." Reggie held open the door and waited while Brooke gathered her things.

"You're sure it'll be safe here?"

"Yes. They have a night guard that patrols both garages. It's as safe as anywhere in Dallas."

A few minutes later, they were on their way to Brooke's house. It wasn't a flirty ice cream date, but Reggie was happy to have the time alone with her and suddenly cared a whole lot less about all the studying she had left to do.

CHAPTER EIGHT

That's me." Brooke pointed at the apartment complex up ahead. "I really appreciate the ride. You can let me out here." She practically hugged the door in her hurry to exit. The ride should've been a pleasant opportunity to get to know Reggie better, but she'd been too preoccupied with worry that the man from the garage or one of his cohorts would see her doing exactly what she'd been told not to do and take action.

"Are you sure? I can get you closer if you want."

She did want and bailing out of the car a block away seemed rude, like she was trying to hide where she lived from Reggie. And now that she thought about it, she'd been given mixed messages by the mystery man. First, she wasn't supposed to hang out with the other jurors and then she'd been told to sway them to a particular verdict and start laying the groundwork to make that happen. If she was confronted about what she was doing with Reggie, she could simply point out the inconsistency in her assigned mission. She pointed to the turn ahead. "You can pull in there and take the next left."

Reggie followed her instructions and parked in the space reserved for her car. Brooke took her time gathering her things which included the textbooks she usually hauled around with her.

"I appreciate the ride. What do you have planned tonight?" She hadn't planned to ask that question, but now that she had, she desperately wanted to know.

"Nothing exciting. I have studying to do."

"You're in school?"

"Kind of. I'm studying for my private investigator licensing exam. It's coming up soon and I'm not nearly ready."

Brooke held up her marketing text. "Midterm next week. Not ready. At all."

An awkward pause followed, and Brooke's brain filled it with a repeating idea. *Ask her to stay. Ask her to stay. Ask her to stay.* Finally, she blurted out, "Do you want to stay for dinner? We could study after. It won't be anything fancy, but—"

"I'd love to." Reggie reached into the back seat and grabbed a bag. "I'm sick to death of takeout and I could use a different set of walls to stare at when I'm trying to come up with the answers to all the tricky test questions."

Brooke smiled, partly because she was happy Reggie was staying and partly to mask her anxiety. The morning had been such a blur because she'd overslept, she wasn't sure the house was presentable or that she even had any food in the fridge, but it was too late now. Reggie was already out of the car and waiting, so she hefted her books and climbed out.

They were almost to the door when she heard a voice call out her name and she turned to see Mr. Peterson walking toward her with an envelope in his hand. She plastered a smile on her face and prayed he wasn't holding an eviction notice. "Hi, Mr. Peterson."

He took a moment to look Reggie up and down before acknowledging her greeting. "Hi. This came for you." He handed over the envelope. "It was delivered to the main office. I don't have time to deliver stuff, so tell whoever sent it to use the mail like regular folks." He cleared his throat and shot another look at

Reggie. "And I need you to come by and see me tomorrow about that other thing."

"You bet. Happy to do it." She knew her voice was overly enthusiastic and pitched a bit too high, but she was relieved he'd chosen not to bring up the past due rent and too busy willing him to leave to care that she sounded crazy. "See you tomorrow." She waved to punctuate his exit before quickly opening the front door and motioning for Reggie to follow her in.

"Who was that guy?" Reggie asked.

"Landlord. He's a little intense."

"You can say that again."

Brooke shrugged. "The bane of living in an apartment, I guess." She led the way to the kitchen and set her books on the small table in the breakfast nook. "If you want, you can go ahead and get started studying while I sort out dinner."

Reggie set her bag down, but instead of sitting, she joined her in the kitchen. "How about I help sort out dinner and then we can both study."

Brooke's breathing quickened at Reggie's closeness and her thoughts turned from what to cook to how to cool the heat between them. Dinner and studying—that was the focus and anything else was completely off the table. She opened the refrigerator and stuck her head inside. "I confess I haven't been to the store this week. I can make omelets or turkey sandwiches, and that's about it."

"I like omelets and turkey sandwiches," Reggie said, managing to make both options sound like something way more exciting than a meal. "What does your son like?"

"Ben would eat pizza for dinner every night of the week if he could, but given a choice between these two options, he's more of a sandwich guy."

"Then sandwiches it is." Reggie looked around. "Where do you keep the bread?"

Brooke pointed to the pantry across the room, both grateful and sad to send Reggie out of her orbit for a moment so she could compose herself. In the meantime, she pulled condiments, the packet of sliced turkey, and the provolone cheese that Ben liked out of the fridge and set them on the counter. When Reggie returned with the bread, she handed her plates and asked her to set the table.

She'd just started arranging the fixings on a platter when Reggie held up the envelope Peterson had brought over. "This fell on the floor," she said. "Where would you like me to put it?"

She'd been so preoccupied with Reggie's presence, she hadn't paid attention to the fact this envelope looked exactly like the others that had shown up, each carrying threats about the pending trial. Without thinking, she snatched the envelope from Reggie's hand and gripped it tightly. She wanted to rip it open and confront whatever was inside, but she also wanted to burn it and forget it had ever existed. She looked up to see Reggie staring at her with a worried expression.

"Something's wrong."

"No, everything's fine."

"Are you expecting bad news?"

Brooke shook her head afraid if she spoke out loud she wouldn't be able to keep her secret any longer, but Reggie was not to be deterred.

"Wait a minute. You mentioned something about envelopes before. Didn't you accuse me of putting an envelope in your purse? Is someone harassing you? Is it that guy I saw you talking to in the parking garage yesterday?"

Brooke felt the tears start to form and she swiped at her eyes with her hand, determined she wasn't going to cry in front of Reggie who would no doubt think she'd lost her mind. As if it could hear her plea, the universe interrupted with a rousing version of "The Imperial March."

"What's that?" Reggie asked.

Brooke took a deep breath and prayed for composure. "It's my son." She reached for her phone relieved for the interruption. "Hey, kid, where are you?"

"Mom, don't freak out, but I'm at the hospital."

❖

Reggie steered the Jeep into the parking lot at Baylor, hopped out, and snatched the ticket from the valet's hand. Brooke was already running through the hospital doors.

Brooke had barely spoken on their way here, but Reggie had managed to find out Ben had been in a car accident and he'd hit his head on the passenger side door. The officer on scene had called an ambulance and both Ben and the driver had been brought here to be checked out.

She caught up with Brooke at the reception desk in the ER where she was having an animated discussion with the nurse on duty.

"He just called from here so no, he hasn't been released. Besides, he's a minor, so you need my permission for any treatment—that should be a good enough reason to tell me where he is. Right. Freaking. Now."

Reggie touched her elbow and Brooke whirled around, fists clenched and ready to fight. Reggie raised her hands in surrender. "Hey, hey, not looking for a fight." She pointed at her chest. "Support only." She looked over Brooke's head at the nurse. "Seriously, don't keep her waiting. Her kid just called and said he was here waiting on her. His name is Ben Dawson, and he was in a car accident."

The nurse sighed and typed a few keystrokes into her computer. "Sorry about that," she said. "He wasn't released, but he was taken for an X-ray. He should be back down here by now." She pointed to a set of doors to her right. "Go on back and look for room number three."

Brooke shot through the doors and Reggie jogged to catch up. When they reached the room, she saw a lanky kid sitting on the edge of the bed talking to a nurse. Brooke was instantly at his side, gently hugging him, and asking if he was okay. Repeatedly. He insisted he was before launching into a colorful description of the entire incident.

"We were driving down the street and Mia was going the exact speed limit when out of nowhere, this pickup shoots out from another street, blowing through the stop sign, and plows into us."

Reggie watched Brooke stiffen at the description of what must've been a harrowing experience no matter how cool Ben was trying to play it off and she instinctively reached for Brooke's arm again. This time Brooke didn't shake her away, instead she leaned in.

"Who's this?" Ben asked, pointing at her, his tone more curious than accusatory.

"I'm a friend of your mom's," Reggie spoke first to save Brooke from having to explain why some stranger had showed up at his bedside. "We're serving on a jury together and I was with her when she got the call about your wreck. Is your friend okay?"

"Mia? She's good. The airbag scraped her up a little and her car is pretty messed up, but that's about it." He stuck out his hand. "Ben Dawson. Nice to meet you." He didn't wait for a response before looking over at the nurse. "Can we go now?"

"The doctor has to sign off, but you should be good to go soon." The nurse made a few notes in her tablet and turned to Brooke. "He hit his head, so the doctor's going to want you to keep a close eye on him tonight to make sure he doesn't have a concussion. He had a minor cut that's been cleaned and bandaged, but otherwise he appears to be okay. He will likely be sore tomorrow. If you have any concerns, you can call or bring him back in. Dr. Murphy should be in soon to give you any additional instructions and sign his release."

"Where's Mia?" Brooke asked. "Is she still here?"

"She's in the room next door. Also fine considering. The paramedics said it was quite an impact."

"Do you know if the other driver was hurt?" Reggie asked.

"He took off," Ben said. "Backed up, spun out, and blew down the street like he was being chased by aliens. White, Ford F150, running boards and a charcoal gray bed cover. Texas plates, but I only saw the last three numbers, four six seven."

"That's pretty amazing, Ben."

"I have a head for numbers. I'm a mathlete. If you want, you can come to practice sometime and watch Mia and I compete."

Reggie couldn't help but grin at the kid's enthusiasm in the wake of what could've been a disaster, but her mood sombered when she looked over at Brooke and saw tears streaming down her face.

"I'm okay, Mom," Ben said. "Don't cry. Just be glad I wasn't driving, or Seth would be a goner."

His statement elicited a new, louder round of tears, and Reggie raised her eyebrows at Ben. "Was there someone else in the car with you?"

"Seth is our car. He's ancient and probably wouldn't survive a wreck."

"Ah, yes, I've met Seth." Reggie nodded, remembering the unusual moniker for Brooke's car. "He's a bit under the weather right now. I brought your mom here and I'll take you both home."

Ben jumped down from the bed. "Cool. What do you drive?"

The doctor entered the room before Reggie could answer and she stood off to the side while he gave Ben a final examination and provided cursory instructions to follow up on the ones the nurse had already delivered. He answered Brooke's litany of questions and told them they were free to go.

Reggie pulled the Jeep around and picked Brooke and Ben up at the curb. Brooke's tears had dried, but she wasn't saying much. Reggie wanted to comfort her, but she suspected whatever Brooke was feeling ran deeper than the knowledge her son had been involved in a wreck. She resolved to find out more, but in the meantime, she'd do what she could to relieve some of her stress starting with dinner plans. "I vote we have pizza for dinner. Does that sound good to you two?"

Ben bounced on the back seat at the mention of his favorite meal and Brooke mouthed "thank you." Reggie put the car in park and used the app on her phone to order a couple of pizzas from iFratelli's and headed there to pick them up on the way back to Brooke's. Once they were there, she took the keys Brooke handed her, and led her and Ben into the house. She sent Ben to his room to wash up and change, planted Brooke in the recliner in the living room, and went to the kitchen to put away all signs of the dinner they'd been about to prepare when they had gotten the call from the hospital. When she was done, she spotted the envelope Brooke's landlord had delivered earlier. She tucked it into one of the cabinets and made a mental note to bring it up after Ben had gone to bed.

She and Ben devoured the pizza while Brooke merely nibbled at the edges. After dinner Ben read aloud the doctor's orders and sent himself to bed, making Reggie promise she'd administer the hourly checks to make sure his eyes weren't dilated. She shot a look at Brooke but didn't get a signal either way about her feelings on the matter, so she agreed. It meant she'd have to spend the night, but that recliner looked pretty comfortable, and besides, Ben and Brooke would need rides in the morning since Seth the Subaru was out of commission.

Reggie shooed Brooke back to the living room, and then put the dishes in the dishwasher and stowed the leftover pizza in the oven. She retrieved the envelope from the cabinet and joined Brooke who was staring at the blank screen on the TV.

"I'm sorry I've checked out on you," Brooke said. "This day has been really extra."

"It has, but don't worry about me. I'm just glad Ben is okay."

"For now."

Reggie wasn't sure how to react to the ominous statement, but she had a hunch. "Brooke, I get the feeling you think Ben and Mia's car wreck wasn't an accident."

"It wasn't."

"And you know that because?"

Brooke turned to face her, her eyes red and swollen. "I just know."

Reggie held up the envelope. "Does it have something to do with this?"

Brooke's features froze. "Yes."

"You haven't even opened it."

"I don't need to." Brooke jabbed a finger at it. "You do it. Please."

Reggie hesitated, taking a minute to study Brooke's face until she came to a decision. This wasn't a trap. Brooke needed her to take this step on her behalf and it was the least she could do. She gently edged the envelope open and eased out the card inside. Colorful block letters that looked like they'd been cut from a magazine spelled out the message:

You were warned. Don't disobey again.

She picked up the envelope again and stared inside. There was nothing else there. She studied the card, front and back. The message was straightforward, but it didn't mean anything without context. Warned about what?

"Do you want to see it?" she asked Brooke.

"Let me guess. It says something about me breaking the rules, not doing what I've been told. There will be consequences."

"Pretty much. I'm thinking this is not the first message like this you've received."

"It's not." Brooke leaned forward, reaching for the note and Reggie handed it to her. Brooke read it several times before setting it on the coffee table. "Before you ask, I don't know who's sending these. It's probably the man who you saw me talking to in the parking garage, but his face was hidden, so I wouldn't be able to ID him."

"Do you know what it means?"

"Yes. It's about the jury. I'm supposed to sway the jury to find Shirley Mitchell not guilty and if I don't, whoever sent this message is going to kill Ben."

Chapter Nine

Reggie dropped Brooke off at the door to the courthouse before parking her Jeep in the garage. She'd stayed up all night thinking about the threats Brooke had received and wondering what they were going to do about them because doing nothing wasn't an option. Over coffee, she'd gently encouraged Brooke to take the notes to the police, but Brooke had vehemently stated there was no way she was going to risk that move.

They'd had a lively conversation about the subject all the way to the courthouse. Brooke kept pointing out that if she'd simply followed the instructions she'd been given and not been talking to her outside of court, Ben and his friend Mia wouldn't have been in danger. No matter how hard she tried, Reggie couldn't get her to see that whoever was threatening her wasn't going to stop no matter what she did to comply. Anyone who would threaten a child had no moral compass and there was nothing to prevent them from taking further action. Brooke had remained unswayed.

Which meant she'd have to act on her own and she knew exactly where to start.

She started by calling Leroy and telling him she had an emergency this morning and she would be about an hour late. He groused, but he'd known her a long time and took her at her word.

She felt a little guilty about that, but not guilty enough to change her course. Next she sent a text to Lennox. *Need an emergency consult. You, Judge A, Skye. Off campus. Name the place.*

She set the phone down and waited. A full, agonizing minute later, Lennox texted her back. *Riverside Diner. See you in ten.*

She started the Jeep and headed to the diner which was less than a quarter mile from the courthouse. It would be packed by lunchtime, but at this time of day, most of its clientele were already at the courthouse deep into the morning docket. She drove around the parking lot three times to make sure she didn't spot anyone suspicious, and finally deciding it was safe, she parked her Jeep and headed inside setting up at a booth with a full view of the parking lot.

"Coffee, hun?"

She didn't recognize the waitress, but she looked like all the others who worked here—mid-fifties, pen nestled in a big bun, notepad at the ready. She turned over the mug on the table. "Yes, please. Black. I'm waiting on some people."

While the waitress fetched her coffee, Reggie scoped out the place. Besides a woman with a baby sitting across the room, she was the only one there. Her phone pinged with a text.

Where are you? The bailiff said you had an emergency.

She wanted to answer Brooke, but there was nothing she could safely say in a text to her to explain her absence and a lie could get them both in trouble, so she stowed her phone in her pocket and hoped she'd have some answers by the time she saw Brooke again.

A minute later Lennox, followed by Wren, Skye, Judge Aguilar, and her girlfriend, Franco burst through the door. The waitress appeared with a pot of coffee at the same time they reached her table.

"These your people?" she asked. Reggie nodded. "Then you're going to need a bigger table." She motioned for the group to follow her to the other end of the restaurant, even farther from the other occupied table and she pointed at a large booth. "That should do. Menu's on the table." She poured coffee for everyone who wanted it and hustled back to the kitchen.

"I see you brought reinforcements," Reggie said to Lennox.

"You said it was an emergency. This is the best group of folks I know when it comes to emergencies. What's up?"

Reggie took a deep breath. It was one thing to think about enlisting her friends' help, but it was entirely different now that they were sitting in front of her waiting to hear what she needed and why. Whatever she said next, she was breaking her promise to Brooke to keep her secret, but surely Brooke had known she wouldn't be able to sit by and do nothing. It was a risk she had to take. "Let's start with a hypothetical. Say a juror is being intimidated to vote a certain way and also influence other jurors to do the same."

"You should report it," Lennox said.

"It's not me."

"Doesn't matter. If you know about it, you should report it to the judge."

"Okay." Reggie drew out the word. "Now, let's say that the juror has received a threat against a family member if the juror doesn't comply."

"Same," Lennox said, folding her arms across her chest as if the matter was closed.

"Wait," Wren said, placing a hand on Lennox's shoulder. "Take a breath, Crime Crusader. Reggie's right, the threat changes things. Reggie, tell us more about these threats."

"Altered voice on the phone, cards with serial killer style notes delivered to the juror's house or left in the juror's belongings."

"That definitely makes it more complicated," Wren said. "And this juror, they think the threats are real?"

Reggie shook her head. "Absolutely. With good reason. The family member who was threatened wound up in a car wreck with a hit-and-run driver last night that didn't sound much like an accident."

"Are you okay?" Judge Aguilar asked. "Are you the juror?"

Reggie shook her head. "I swear it's not me. I'm fine." She paused. "There's another thing." She waited until she had their rapt attention. "They started getting the threats before they showed up for jury duty. Right after they got the summons."

"So, someone knew they'd been selected to be on the panel," Nina said. "That narrows it down a bit, but there are still quite a few people who might have access to the list of people who'd received a summons for any given day."

"True, but how would they have any way of knowing they'd get called to Hunt's court and actually make the cut?" Wren asked.

"That's the thing," Reggie said. "They didn't. Not at first." She described how Mr. Rodriguez had collapsed on his way to the jury box, opening the last spot for Brooke, and as she recounted the story, her heart started pumping as her blood pressure started to rise.

"You think someone tried to take out a juror to give them a spot?" Lennox asked. "That's pretty ballsy and a huge risk. How would they have known she'd be next in line? It's almost like someone had to be in the room, calling the shots as it went down."

They all sat in silence for a moment, digesting Lennox's words. Reggie had been turning the same thought over and over in her head since Brooke had told her everything the night before, but no matter how many times she went over it, she couldn't come up with how someone had made it happen.

"New question," Franco said, waving her hand in the air. "Does this juror have any idea why they were singled out, assuming they are the only one being intimidated on this particular jury?"

"They don't, but I have a theory." Reggie hesitated for a moment and then decided to go ahead and say what she knew. "Single parent, trying to finish a degree while working a full-time job. More vulnerable than most. When their kid is threatened, they didn't have anyone close to turn to, so it's easier to comply."

"Makes sense," Judge Aguilar said. "This person is on the same jury as you?"

"Yes."

"What are you going to do?"

"Well, that's kind of why I asked you all here. I'm not sure what to do. I don't want to put them in danger, but I know this has to be reported. Does me telling you count?"

Nina laughed. "Nice try. You're in the middle of a trial and both sides have a right to know if the other is tampering with the jury. You're going to have to tell the judge."

"Wait a minute," Skye said. "Wouldn't it be better if you caught whoever this is in the act? What if you let the trial keep going and lay a trap? The trial's going to end up in a mistrial anyway. What's a few more days so you have a chance to heap on bigger charges?" She turned to Lennox. "Can't the DA's office run an investigation without anyone knowing about it?"

"It's complicated. Someone could say we did it to tank this particular case. We could report it to law enforcement and let them lay the trap." She turned to Nina. "Judicial opinion, please?"

"You're right," Nina said. "It is complicated. Judge me says you should report it to Judge Hunt right away, but former prosecutor me knows that's going to result in a mistrial and the offender might never be caught. Lennox, what if you call the local FBI office to see if they can put someone on it—that way it's as far removed from your office as possible?"

Lennox nodded. "That's actually not a bad idea."

"Hold up." Reggie leaned forward. "I invited you all here for advice not to sit back and watch this turn into a federal agent shit show. Besides, she was specifically told not to contact law enforcement. What happens when whoever's watching her finds out the freaking FBI is on the scene?" She shook a fist to emphasize her point, but her friends merely stared at her in silence. "What?"

Lennox was the first to speak. "'Her'?"

Damn. She'd let the pronoun slip. She kept her mouth shut to avoid revealing more.

"Are you sure it's not you," Nina asked, her eyes narrowed with skepticism.

"A million percent. Can we focus on the 'in danger' part of the equation, please?"

"You like her, don't you?"

"Knock it off, Lennox." Reggie said the words with a low growl.

"I get it," Lennox said as she put her hand on Wren's. "Now fess up that you like her and we'll move mountains to keep her safe."

She hadn't called the posse here to bail out a girlfriend and this conversation was taking a turn she hadn't prepared for. She'd come here looking for help for a fellow human being who was in trouble, not for the personal gain that would come from helping someone she was crushing on because she definitely wasn't crushing on Brooke. Not even.

Well, maybe just a little bit.

It was kind of hard not to.

Still, she wasn't about to admit that to Lennox or anyone else seated around this table. "Look, do you want to help me out or not?"

Lennox let loose a heavy sigh. "Of course. Look, it's classic bad guy to say 'don't involve the police,' but that rarely means they'll do anything about it or even know the cops are involved. I worked on a task force case last year with an FBI agent who knows her way around. What if I reach out to her and see if she has any ideas?"

"I want to be there when you talk to her," Reggie said, thinking she could hang on to some modicum of control if she was in the room.

"Wouldn't want it any other way. I'll see if I can set something up tonight."

Reggie turned to Nina. "What am I supposed to do in the meantime?" She looked at her watch. "I sent Leroy a text this morning to tell him I was running late, but there's only so long he can hold the judge off from tossing me in the holdover. I should get back." She left unsaid the reason, which was to keep watch over Brooke, but she could tell from the looks she was getting that the others knew exactly why she wanted to get back.

Nina made a shooing motion. "Go. Lennox will call you later and if you get any flack about being late from Hunt, let me know and I'll handle it."

Reggie slid out of the booth. "Thanks, guys. I don't know what I'd do without you." As she walked to the door, a deep feeling of loss settled over her. When this trial was over and she was no longer at the courthouse every day, she'd likely lose touch with these folks. Who would she turn to then?

❖

Brooke looked up at the sound of the door opening, but like the dozen other times this morning, there was no Reggie in sight. Where was she? Reggie had dropped her at the courthouse and promptly disappeared.

She'd spotted Leroy, the bailiff, in a whispered conversation with the judge before he'd let them know that they would be starting late this morning due to "other matters before the court," but she couldn't help but wonder if Reggie's absence was the cause for the delay.

"Where's your friend?"

She turned to find Mark standing behind her. "Who?" she asked even though she knew exactly who he meant.

"The woman who acts like a cop and used to work here at the courthouse. I think she likes you."

His words were delivered in a monotone recitation without a drop of judgmental inflection, but Brooke felt seen and it was pretty uncomfortable. She looked around the room, wondering if anyone else had heard Mark's remarks, but he beat her to the punch.

"I don't think anyone else notices," he said. "Your other friends are focused on themselves."

Again, there was no judgment in his tone, but Brooke instantly knew he was talking about Jennifer and Lisa and she choked back a laugh. "Anyone ever tell you you're really observant?"

"Yes, but they don't usually mean it as a compliment. Do you?"

"I do." Brooke smiled to emphasize her point. "It's always the quiet ones." She dropped her voice to a whisper. "What else have you noticed?"

It was his turn to look around, before leaning in to whisper back. "I think you're worried about something. Are you okay?"

She'd expected him to share some revelation about the players in the trial or one of the other jurors, but the pointed observation about her own behavior took her off guard. "Uh, yes, of course," she replied, wondering if Mark was also a deft lie detector. "Guess I'm just like everyone else—I have other things I need to be doing."

He hunched his shoulders. "Not me. I work at the most boring job ever. This is the most interesting thing I've done in a while even if the pay sucks."

She fished through her memories of jury selection. "You work in IT."

He sighed. "I work a customer service line for people who can't figure out their computers. I spend most of my time telling people to turn it off and turn it back on. Not much in the way of intellectually challenging." He pointed to the coffee maker on the counter. "At least here I get free coffee."

"True." She hefted the mug she'd filled when she arrived. "Free coffee is not to be scoffed at."

"Do you think she's going to show up? Your friend, I mean."

His focus on Reggie unnerved her and she wasn't sure why since she was singularly focused on Reggie herself. "I don't know."

"She could be in big trouble if she doesn't."

Brooke resisted looking at her phone. If Reggie had texted or called, it would've buzzed in her hand. The silence was telling, but she wasn't entirely sure she understood the message. Frankly, she was starting to get worried. Had whoever been watching her decided Reggie was a threat?

As if in answer to her question, the door to the jury room opened again and Reggie walked into the room. She was smiling and strolling and seemed utterly unconcerned about the fact she was an hour late. She was two steps away and Brooke was still scrambling for something to say, but she needn't have worried because Reggie walked right on by and struck up a conversation with Jennifer and Lisa who greeted her like they were long-lost friends. Brooke continued to stare and, at one point, Reggie met her eyes and quickly glanced away, her expression unreadable. She hadn't imagined that, had she?

"She's back."

Mark's observation dropped like a rock. Yes, Reggie was back, but something was different; something was off from their easy back-and-forth this morning. This Reggie wasn't the same person she'd ridden to the courthouse with this morning or the one who'd comforted Ben at the hospital, or her at her house. This version acted like she didn't exist.

She was trying to decide between ignoring Reggie too or confronting her when Leroy appeared at the door.

"Judge's ready for y'all. And he asked me to make sure you know that we're on a tight schedule for the rest of the day. Everybody make sure to come back from breaks on time."

He glanced at Reggie and squinted like he was tossing emphasis her way. Brooke followed his gaze, and for a brief second Reggie smiled, but she wasn't certain if the friendly overture was for her or merely in response to Leroy's gentle admonition, and with a busy day ahead, she doubted she was going to find out anytime soon.

The first witness of the day was another one of Shirley Mitchell's business acquaintances. The prosecutor spent a lot of time trying to get him to say Shirley had tried to get him involved in a scheme with her, but he never quite went there and kept throwing uncomfortable glances in Shirley's direction as if to say, "what have you gotten us involved in?" Brooke was laser-focused on his behavior and couldn't help but wonder if he was under the same kind of pressure she was. Rigley finally passed the witness and sat down, visibly frustrated at the lack of cooperation from a witness he'd chosen to call to the stand.

Leland took her time starting her cross-examination, spending a few moments staring at a piece of paper in front of her like it contained the secrets of the universe. When she finally looked up at the witness, her expression was almost feral. "You look uncomfortable to be sitting there, Mr. Ross."

Ross bit his lip and looked down.

"Nothing to say?" Leland taunted him. "Wait. Let me rephrase that. Why do you look so uncomfortable, Mr. Ross?"

This time he straightened his shoulders and looked directly at her. Brooke flinched inwardly at the daggers in his eyes and held her breath for his answer, but after a moment, his bravado deflated, and he looked down at his hands.

"I'm not," he said.

"Okay, then." Again with the exaggerated smile. "Let's get to it." Leland picked up the paper she'd been studying. "How many deals have you done with Ms. Mitchell over the past ten years?"

He shrugged. "I'd have to consult my records to determine the exact amount."

"More than five?"

"Probably."

"More than ten?"

He shifted in his seat again. "I'm not sure of the exact amount."

"So somewhere between five and so many that you can't remember the amount."

Rigley shot out of his seat. "Objection, Judge. Defense counsel is testifying."

Brooke stared at Leland who raised her hands in surrender. "I withdraw the question." She turned to look at the jury and rolled her eyes. "Mr. Ross, did the prosecutors meet with you to prepare for your testimony here at trial?"

Again with the shifting. "We talked so they could give me a general idea of what to expect."

"And they asked you questions, asked you about your interactions with Ms. Mitchell?"

"Sure, but—"

"Is it your testimony that no one in the DA's office asked you how many deals you've done with Ms. Mitchell?"

His eyes darted around the room, but there was no escape from the cage of her questions. He shot a quick look at the jury before plunging in. "I'm sure they asked. They asked a bunch of things. That doesn't mean I remember every little thing or the answer I gave."

"Makes perfect sense," Leland said. "You'd have to check your records, like you said."

"Yes, that's right." He relaxed back into his chair looking relieved that Leland finally got him.

Leland reached into a briefcase sitting next to her chair and pulled out a stack of bound notebooks. She shuffled them into a different order and stood. "Your Honor, may I approach?"

"You may, counselor," he said.

She was already on the move, dropping a set of bound notebooks on the prosecutor's table before striding to the witness stand. She handed a set to Ross. "I had a feeling you might need these so I brought them along. Please describe to the jury what I've handed to you."

He took a moment to examine the notebooks. His expression barely changed, but Brooke recognized the tightness in his shoulders and his pale face as signs he knew he was navigating a mine field. She should know. When he finally spoke, the trepidation in his voice was clear.

"There's a lot to sift through here."

"Indeed," Leland said. "But I made sure to organize the files you provided to the ADA." She pointed at a tab. "The list of cases you worked with Ms. Mitchell is right there. Please read it to the jury."

The next few moments were painful as Ross reluctantly recounted deal after deal he'd worked with Shirley Mitchell during the last decade, and Brooke had to admit she admired Leland's technique. If Ross had simply admitted the amount up front, it wouldn't have had the same impact as his painful recitation. As he droned on, Brooke focused her attention on Shirley Mitchell and wondered how deeply Shirley was involved in the threats she'd received. Voice-changing device or not, she didn't think this powerful, confident woman had called her on the phone or cut out letters in a magazine to frame a threatening missive, but she had to be aware someone was working to sway the jury on her behalf, right? Was that why she looked so cool, so calm—because she knew her fate and it was freedom?

Ross finally stopped reading and Brooke refocused her attention to the front of the room where Leland was practically salivating.

"I counted twenty-four deals," Leland said. "Does that sound about right to you?"

"I guess so." Ross spoke with quiet defeat. Brooke looked over at the prosecutors who looked like they were trying too hard to hide their disappointment, and a nagging question surfaced.

If things were going so well for the defense, then why was she being threatened into swaying the jury to find Shirley Mitchell not guilty?

CHAPTER TEN

Reggie saw Brooke walking toward her and started to duck out of the jury room, but Brooke spotted her before she could make her escape.

"Hey," Brooke said.

"Hey." Reggie stuck her hands in her pockets and glanced toward the door while Brooke followed her gaze. Lennox had set up a meeting with the FBI agent she knew, and she only had a few minutes to make it downtown. She should've prepared for this moment. After all, she'd driven Brooke to the courthouse that morning, it was only natural for Brooke to assume she'd drive her home, but it was too soon to loop Brooke into her plan.

"I called for an Uber."

"Oh." Brooke's words should've released her guilt, but instead she felt worse. Brooke hadn't assumed they'd ride home together, maybe didn't even want to spend more time with her. She'd been a jerk to assume she would.

"You seemed distracted today," Brooke said. "I figured you needed to deal with some stuff on your own and I can take care of myself."

"Look, I want to talk more about what you told me this morning." Reggie looked at the door again. "But I need to take care of something first. Can I call you later?"

"I don't think it's a good idea." Brooke backed away and almost struck the wall behind her before she veered toward the door. "Thanks for the ride this morning and for being there for me last night, but I'm good now."

Reggie watched her walk away, anxious to correct the misunderstanding, but knowing it was even more important to keep Brooke safe while she tried to subvert the threat she was under.

Twenty minutes later, she arrived at the FBI office on the third floor of the federal building downtown and checked in with the receptionist. Lennox showed up a minute later.

"Tell me you did what you promised," Reggie said before Lennox even crossed the threshold of the reception area.

"I said I would and I did." Lennox signed the visitor log and sat down next to her. "I had to call in a few favors, but she'll have a cop assigned to keep an eye on her place at night. It was the best I could do."

"And they'll be discreet?"

"Yes." Lennox cocked her head. "Are you sure you didn't know this woman before you wound up on a jury together?"

Reggie shook her head. She'd known Lennox a long time—they'd even briefly dated at one point—and she knew she could trust her discretion, but she didn't have a good answer for what Lennox really wanted to know which was why she was so invested in Brooke's fate. It definitely went beyond a desire to see justice be done, but she wasn't ready to try other reasons out loud.

"Look," Lennox said. "I get it. We've been through a lot the last few months. It would be nice to see someone have to pay for what they've done."

"Yes, it would." Reggie fished for another subject. "Any word on your brother's case?"

"There's a hearing scheduled in a few weeks, but I don't know that it'll go anywhere." Lennox sighed. "I know in my gut that Harry Benton had something to do with Daniel being set up, but I don't know that we'll ever be able to prove it. If only Gloria hadn't talked Daniel into taking a plea, we'd be in a much better position to overturn the plea and get him a trial." She paused. "Sorry, I guess I shouldn't be bad-mouthing my ex when you're a juror on a case she's defending."

"I think we've crossed so many lines already, that one barely matters."

Before Lennox could respond, a dark-haired woman poked her head through the door next to the reception desk. "Lennox, you ready?"

"You bet." Lennox stood and motioned to Reggie. "This is Reggie Knoll. Reggie, meet Special Agent Sarah Flores."

They followed Sarah back through the offices to a small room in the corner and sat down around a tiny desk. "I thought the ADA's offices were small," Reggie said. "I would expect you to have better digs."

"Budget cuts. You should see what the less senior agents have to deal with." Sarah jerked her chin in Lennox's direction. "So, you work at the courthouse with this one?"

Reggie glanced over at Lennox, wishing they'd taken the time to work out an approach before barreling in here. Lennox merely nodded, so she decided to plunge right in. "Used to. I'm in between gigs right now, but I wound up on Shirley Mitchell's jury and that's what we're here to talk to you about."

Sarah leaned back in her chair, her face a mask of nonchalance, but Reggie noticed she started twirling the pen in her hand like it was one of those fidget spinners. She was interested in hearing more. Very.

"Someone's threatening at least one of the jurors," Lennox said. "We have reason to think the threats are real."

"Do you now?" Sarah crossed her arms. "Lennox, should you even be here without opposing counsel?"

"It's not my case."

"I thought all cases at the DA's office belong to the entire office."

"Technically, yes, but sometimes we have to deal with cases that cross the line. This is one of those."

"And you're trying to drag me across the line with you?"

"Shirley Mitchell has a lot of contracts for federal public housing. If she's in so much trouble that she's threatening a juror, you can bet there are problems with her federal projects as well. Don't you want a chance to take her down?"

Reggie watched while Lennox stared Sarah down, and after a few moments of silence, she decided she was tired of their back-and-forth. "The threats are real. I know it for a fact. Somebody needs to do something, and I don't really care which one of you it is."

Sarah raised her eyebrows, but Lennox flashed a hint of a smile which she quickly hid by placing a hand in front of her face.

"Say I take you up on this challenge," Sarah asked. "What do you propose that I do?"

Now it was her turn to stare at Sarah while she reviewed and promptly dismissed every idea that came to mind. It was fine in the abstract to imagine a targeted operation designed to capture Shirley Mitchell, or whoever was working on her behalf, in the act of coercing a juror, but it was a whole different story trying to come up with a way to trick her into revealing her culpability

"Look, I'm not the one in a position to know," she said. "I'm a regular citizen stuck on a case, reporting an incident of jury tampering." She wagged a finger between Sarah and Lennox. "You two are the ones who are supposed to come up with the ideas about how to bring the bad guys to justice." She paused and faced Sarah. "Do you really mean to tell me the bureau hasn't been investigating Shirley Mitchell? Don't you have some leverage you can use with the DA's office to get her to take a deal? If she did, this trial would be over, and the threat gone. Everyone wins."

"So, you don't care about her being prosecuted for making the threats—you only want the threats to stop?"

Sarah delivered the question with narrowed eyes, like she didn't fully trust her motives, and Reggie didn't blame her. She should want Shirley to go down for putting Brooke's son in danger, but the truth was they might not ever prove she had anything to do with it. People like Shirley always had lackeys with misplaced loyalties who were willing to take the fall or take action to insulate their boss, and for all she knew Shirley might not know any of the details of the things that had been done on her behalf. But if the DA's office could work out a deal to get her to plead guilty instead of continuing with the trial, Brooke would no longer be in danger and she could get back to her life. "I want whatever makes the most sense, and right now that seems like a plea. It's a win for the DA's office and will keep the rest of the jurors safe."

Sarah sighed and looked at Lennox. "Is everyone you know a bleeding heart?"

Lennox replied with a shrug. "Maybe. She's not wrong though. You have the resources to make this work."

"The real question," Reggie added, "is whether you have the guts to make it happen." She held her breath as she waited for Sarah's answer. If she wasn't willing to take on the case, they'd be back to square one and she'd have to figure out a way to protect Brooke on her own. Not ideal, but maybe sorting out the truth was a worthy substitute for studying for her PI exam. She squared her shoulders and waited for Sarah's answer. Whatever it was, she was ready, and she'd do whatever was necessary to keep Brooke safe.

❖

Brooke dropped her keys twice while trying to unlock the door to her apartment, and she vowed to dropkick them across the complex if they didn't work on the next turn. Thankfully, they complied and she pushed open the door and dropped her purse on the table just inside.

"Hi, Mom."

She looked across the room at Ben who was sitting in front of the TV munching on handfuls of Cheetos with orange-tipped fingers. "Hey, kiddo. Make sure you don't rub any of that on the couch, okay?"

"Sure, Mom." He punctuated the response by rolling his eyes and, instead of finding it as annoying as always, she breathed a sigh of relief at the very normal preteen sign of disrespect because it signaled he wasn't sitting around fretting about what had happened to him. "Can we get burgers from Jake's for dinner?"

Burgers sounded great and totally worth blowing the last bit of cash she had on hand, but then she remembered. "Sorry, pal. I'm still without a car and they're not on any of the apps. Does Shake Shack work for you?"

"Bummer, but yeah the Shack'll do."

He turned back to his show as if she'd disappeared in a puff of smoke. If only she could set aside the circumstances and act as nonchalant about the circumstances. If only she knew what the circumstances were. Maybe it was time to figure that out on her own.

She placed the order, trying not to flinch at the fees, and then fished around in one of the kitchen drawers. When you were about to list all the ways your life was messed up, pen and paper seemed like the way to go. She finally located a pen from the auto shop that had taken most of her savings last month, and a Post-it pad she'd swiped from the restaurant, deciding it would have to do. At the top of one of the Post-its she wrote: *Reasons To Leave Town.* She started to scratch it out, but decided instead it was a decent code for her feelings about her current options.

Talk to the judge
Go to the police
Sway the jury

She stared at the list for several minutes. She didn't like the order and she didn't like the options, but they were all she had. With the first two, she might be able to shut this whole thing down sooner, but the risk was high. The risk was high with the last option too since she wasn't convinced she could sway anyone on the jury, but all she really had to do was hold out. A hung jury wasn't going to please the voice on the phone because Mitchell could be tried again, but it was better than a conviction.

"Mom, the food's here," Ben bellowed from the living room. "They're almost at the door and I'm finishing my homework."

"Be right there." Brooke decided to let him have a pass on getting the door after what he'd been through. Another reason option number three was looking better and better. She crumpled the Post-it and tossed it in the trash. She knew what she had to do if she wanted to keep her little family safe and get back to her life as soon as possible. The only problem remaining was the fact she'd told Reggie about the threats. Reggie didn't strike her as the kind of person who would just let things go, but she wasn't sure what she was going to do about it.

When she swung open the door to collect the food, Reggie was standing there holding the Shake Shack bag. "What are you doing here?" Brooke stammered the words feeling like she'd conjured Reggie's presence and wishing she'd had time to prepare before seeing her again.

Reggie shifted in place and looked sheepish. "Well, I could lie and say I work food delivery at night, but the truth is I tipped the delivery guy to get him to give me the food so I'd have an excuse to see you. May I come in?"

Brooke's heart quickened at the idea Reggie wanted to see her again, but she took a few deep breaths to put things in perspective. This was not a social call. "Whatever you have to say, you can say it out here. Ben is home and I don't want him upset after what he's been through."

"Is he okay? Sore, I bet."

Brooke wanted to ignore the question and hurry this encounter along, but Reggie's concern sounded genuine, and she had been there for her during an incredibly stressful time. She held the door open. "Come in, but not for long. Ben has homework and I have things to do."

Reggie grinned and walked inside. She paused in the small foyer and handed over the bag of food. "Good choice," she said, pointing at the bag. "They're definitely in my top ten list of burgers."

"Only you and my son have a top ten list." Brooke peered out the door viewer. "Are you sure you weren't followed?"

"I wasn't." Reggie was emphatic. "I wouldn't put you in danger."

"I don't think you'd do it on purpose, but I don't think you understand the level of risk here." She glanced toward the living room, but Ben was deeply engrossed in whatever was on TV and didn't look remotely interested in their conversation. "He's all I have. This trial is going to wind up costing me work and the ability to pay the bills, and that's without having my and my son's life threatened. I have to do whatever will keep my family safe."

"I know."

Brooke took in a gulp of air. "You do?" She'd been fully prepared to do battle to defend her pronouncement, but it was hard to fight with someone who wasn't fighting back.

"Absolutely. That's why I'm here. I have a plan."

Brooke wanted to believe her. She wanted to believe there was a way out that didn't involve her helping a criminal go free because even if Shirley hadn't committed the crimes she was accused of, she had done worse by not only threatening her son, but making good on that threat with little provocation. But the same reasons that motivated her to believe in Reggie also held her back from trusting anyone to help her out of this mess. She looked into Reggie's eyes, fully prepared to tell her she wanted no part of any plan, but Reggie's earnest smile and encouraging eyes coaxed her into hearing more. She shook the bag in her hand. "Food first and then the plan."

A few minutes later, the three of them sat around the kitchen table, munching on burgers and fries. Reggie had resisted taking half of Brooke's food, but she'd insisted because she wasn't that hungry, which was true. She hadn't had much of an appetite since this whole mess had started. Ben and Reggie, on the other hand, devoured their food, taking bites between a lively discussion about the latest Comic Con that had been in Dallas.

"*Walking Dead*'s not my favorite show, but I love Eugene," Ben said.

"Eugene's great, but I'm more of a Maggie fan."

"The women in the show are badass," Ben said, immediately covering his mouth.

Brooke gave him a side-eye punctuated by a grin. "The women in that show are indeed badass, but that's the only context in which you're allowed to use that word until you're much older. Got it?"

"Got it."

Ben stuffed the last of his fries in his mouth, unfazed by the admonition. Brooke wasn't worried. He was a good kid who might occasionally violate the rules in an attempt to seem cool, but she was confident he'd make good choices when it really mattered. "Hey, kid, go finish your homework. I need to talk to Reggie alone for a bit."

"'Kay," he said, sliding out of his chair and taking his plate to the sink. "Nice to see you again, Reggie."

"Nice to see you too, Ben."

Brooke watched the exchange and shook her head.

"What is it?" Reggie asked.

"You're good with him."

Reggie laughed. "It's pretty darn easy. I simply challenge my inner twelve-year-old who is much more present than the adult version on most days."

"Don't downplay it. You have a real talent when it comes to relating to kids. A lot of parents don't have those skills."

Reggie shrugged. "Ben is easy to get along with and he's a likable kid."

They sat for a moment in silence while Brooke tried to figure out how to bring the subject around to Reggie's plan. Part of her didn't want to hear it at all. She already had a plan. Do what she was told and hope for the best. It wasn't the greatest, but it was probably less risky than anything Reggie was about to propose. "About that plan," she started before Reggie cut in.

"Promise you'll at least hear me out before you say it isn't going to work."

She didn't want to. There was no reason she should trust this woman she barely knew. But as she stared into Reggie's eyes, she saw something she'd given up on ever having—a person who genuinely cared about her and who was taking risks to make sure she and her son stayed safe. She wasn't quite ready to trust the vulnerability that went with the realization, but she didn't see what harm could come from simply listening to what Reggie had to say.

"I promise."

CHAPTER ELEVEN

Reggie paced the room, growing more nervous with each pass. Brooke should've been here twenty minutes ago.

"Are you sure she's going to show up?" Sarah asked, echoing her thoughts.

"I think so."

"You think so? Come on, Knoll. I opened a case to help out your girl, but if she doesn't show up, we both look stupid."

"Lay off, Flores," Lennox said. "You know you opened the case to be the star that gets to take down Shirley Mitchell. Give her a minute."

Reggie mouthed a silent "thank you" to Lennox and continued to pace. She was on her second pass by the door when it flung open in her path and Brooke burst into the room.

"Freaking Uber driver kept trying to go to the wrong courthouse. I'm sorry I'm late."

Reggie grabbed her hand and squeezed. "It's okay. You're here now."

"I am, but I'm still not sure I'm on board with this plan."

Brooke looked down at their hands which were still joined, and Reggie followed her gaze. She should care that Lennox and this FBI agent she barely knew were staring at them, but all she felt in the moment was the warmth of Brooke's touch and the easy way their fingers intertwined. "Trust me, okay?"

Several beats of silence followed before Brooke broke the quiet. "I do." She turned to the others who looked away, pretending they hadn't been watching. "Tell me how this is going to work."

Sarah motioned for them to sit down and once they were all settled, she launched in. "The judge is going to call a recess and ask to see the attorneys for both sides in chambers. He'll explain that he has reason to believe someone has been tampering with the jury and that the FBI has launched an investigation, but they will continue with the trial pending the investigation. He won't let on that he knows anything about which direction the jury was being swayed."

"And then what?" Brooke asked.

"And then I'll corner Mitchell's attorney. Let her know her client is the suspect in the tampering case and ask for a few minutes with Mitchell to lay out the case. We'll offer her a deal to come clean."

"You make it sound easy," Reggie said, shooting a look in Brooke's direction to let her know she was on her side. "Someone who would threaten a juror's family and make good on that threat isn't going to fold at the first sign of adversity."

"We're assuming Mitchell knows what's going on," Sarah said. "I mean she's no innocent, but it's possible one of her loyal employees crossed the line without permission from above. She would probably happily trade in one of her minions to save her own ass."

Lennox cleared her throat. "There's another possibility. If I was in Gloria's shoes, which would never happen by the way, I'd ask for a mistrial claiming that if the jury was being tampered with, there's no way my client could get a fair trial. It's the perfect way to fade the heat from her client, and Gloria loves giving a big display of indignation—it's her trademark move."

"So, are you saying we do nothing?"

Everyone turned to stare at Brooke who was clearly over the ruminations. Reggie walked over to her side to signal her support. "Brooke's right. You have to do something and it has to be soon."

"But it can't be a cavalier something," Brooke added. "If your gamble doesn't pay off, you lose a chance at a conviction, but I could lose my son."

The room was quiet for a moment as everyone digested Brooke's words.

"I vote we let Sarah take a crack at Mitchell," Lennox said. "She'll be able to tell if Mitchell's in on it based on her reaction, and if Gloria resorts to histrionics, we'll deal with that when it comes." She turned to Sarah. "What Mitchell does after you talk to her is going to be key. Do you have the resources for surveillance?"

"We'll make it work," Sarah said, looking at Brooke. "You think you can keep it together in the jury room while we do our thing?"

"You've got someone watching Ben?"

"We won't let anything happen to him."

Brooke nodded. "Then do what you need to do."

Reggie squeezed her shoulder and Brooke glanced back, her expression a mix of resolve and fear. She wanted to comfort her, but she wanted to be alone to do it. "Can we have the room, please?"

Lennox and Sarah filed out and she shut the door behind them, waiting a few seconds before asking, "Are you okay?"

"You keep asking me that, but nothing has changed. Ben is still in danger and no one knows who's making the threats. I'll be okay when this is all over."

"Lennox is abrupt, but she knows what she's doing. If she trusts Sarah, then I do too."

"And I trust you."

Reggie could tell it was a big admission and she didn't take it lightly. "I won't do anything to make you doubt that." She reached out a hand. "Shall we go pretend to be jurors for a bit longer?"

Brooke took her hand and stood. "Do you think there's a possibility this could all end today? Maybe Shirley will fess up and we can all go home?"

Reggie looked deeply into Brooke's pleading eyes. She wanted to tell Brooke everything was going to be fine and that there was a good chance her ordeal would be over soon, but the truth was she didn't know, and while she fully supported this plan, it wasn't without risks. If Mitchell did know what was going on, she had the resources and connections to crush Brooke and her son, especially if she was backed into a corner with no other way out. Hell, her developer pal Harry Benton had personally gone after a judge when he was on the verge of being found out for his crimes.

But telling Brooke any of these thoughts would only make her more stressed than she already was. "Yes, there's a possibility. I'm going to hope for the best."

Brooke's shoulders relaxed and she sighed. "Thank you."

Thankful the lie had worked, Reggie pointed to the door. "Whatever happens today, I've got you. Okay?"

"Okay."

Brooke looked from her to the closed door and back again before planting a quick, sweet kiss on her cheek. She started to take off, but Reggie clasped her wrist and pulled her back into her arms. For a few silent moments, they stood close, and Reggie felt Brooke's heart rate quicken, slow, and quicken again, perhaps due to the stress she was under, but maybe, just maybe, Brooke was feeling a hint of the attraction that was beginning to consume her as well.

She wasn't sure who broke contact first, but the void that opened as they stepped away from each other was vast and she instantly missed their closeness. Maybe this ordeal *would* wrap up today and she could explore these feelings. Would Brooke want the same once things returned to normal? She shook her head. She had to believe the attraction between them was born out of more than adversity.

She hoped Brooke believed it too.

❖

It was almost impossible to listen to anything any of the witnesses said. Their voices were a low hum against the backdrop of worry churning through her gut, and Brooke wasn't sure she was going to make it through the rest of the day.

After this morning's meeting with Agent Flores and ADA Roy, she'd gone to the jury room alone to avoid arousing suspicion and spent the next hour waiting around while the judge spoke with the attorneys in chambers. Lisa and Jenny played a guessing game about whether the sides were about to reach a plea deal or if they were arguing over some evidence. They'd tried to engage her, but she wasn't in the mood to play games, and certainly not ones that were more real than anyone in this room besides Reggie even knew.

When they'd finally filed into the courtroom, she'd studiously avoided looking at the defense table at first before realizing not looking might arouse more suspicion than facing them head-on. When she did sneak a look over at Shirley, all she saw was her engaged in what appeared to be a very serious conversation with her attorney, and neither of them seemed to notice she was even in the room. She supposed that was a good thing.

"Are you okay?" Reggie asked in a low whisper.

"You keep asking me that."

"I keep hoping you will be."

"I'm as okay as possible, considering." She could tell by the plea in Reggie's eyes that she'd hoped for more, but she was doing her best to hold it together.

Thankfully, Judge Hunt banged his gavel at that moment, saving her from having to offer assurances she didn't have to give.

"We're going to take our lunch break earlier than usual, but I expect everyone back and ready to go by twelve thirty."

He was out of his seat and through the door before the bailiff could shout "all rise." Brooke followed the rest of the jurors on the trek back to the jury room, pondering a way to find a few moments to herself so she could sort out her thoughts.

"Want to go off campus for a few?" Reggie jangled her keys.

"Actually, I was thinking—" Brooke stopped as Mark joined them, an eager look on his face.

"Did someone say something about getting out of this place for lunch? I'll buy if I can tag along."

It wasn't the scenario she'd envisioned, but including him would keep her from having to talk about anything related to the looming threat and she could use the break. Ignoring Reggie's subtle head shake, she said, "That sounds great. Reggie, do you know a place close by?"

"Uh, sure."

Clearly, Reggie had expected them to dine alone, but Brooke squelched the twinge of guilt and pressed on. "Great. Let's go."

A few minutes later, Reggie pulled her Jeep up to a diner down the street from the courthouse. One of the waitresses waved at Reggie with a friendly smile as they walked in the door.

"Back so soon?" she asked as she led them to a booth in the corner.

Reggie's smile was more of a grimace. "Yep. We have to get back to the courthouse soon. Give us a second and we'll be ready to order." She shot a quick look at Mark who was staring at something outside and didn't appear to notice.

Brooke slid into the booth, curious about the exchange and Reggie's chilly demeanor. She hadn't meant to hurt her feelings by inviting Mark, but she was tired of being the victim who had to be tended to when what she really wanted was to get to know Reggie on equal footing. Maybe when this trial was over, one way or another, they could spend time together without the power imbalance, and she could find out if the closeness she felt was more about real attraction and less about some kind of damsel in distress meets her knight in shining armor scenario.

"I might get the chicken fried steak," Mark announced. He turned to Reggie, his tone eager. "Is it good here?"

Reggie kept her eyes on the menu and her voice was monotone. "I usually order breakfast, but I've heard it's great."

"I'll give it a go," Brooke said, feeling bad now that she'd invited Mark into the middle of a situation he knew nothing about. "I'll even live dangerously and have the fried okra."

After they placed their orders, there were a few uncomfortable moments of silence before Brooke decided to take the reins. "So, Mark, you still think the case is more boring than your job?"

"Mostly. At my job, I at least get to talk to people and take breaks when I want, not when some old dude in a uniform says I can."

"That old dude is in charge of security in the courtroom, and he'd take a bullet for you if he had to."

Brooke stared at Reggie, shocked at her raised voice and the edge of anger behind it. She was certain Mark hadn't meant any harm, but obviously he'd struck a nerve. Instinctively, she reached for Reggie's arm, but stopped herself because she wasn't sure how Reggie would react to her touch with Mark sitting right here watching. Thankfully, the waitress arrived at that moment with their food and the tension in the air dissipated as they focused on their meals.

A few minutes later, Mark waved his fork in the air. "I remember now," Mark said. "You were at the courthouse when the shooting happened. I'm sorry. That must've been rough."

Reggie's shoulders relaxed slightly. "It was. One of the bailiffs almost died trying to save Judge Aguilar's life. Those guys may seem like they're just a bunch of old dudes, but most of them have served a decade or more in law enforcement and they're qualified to do way more than herd a bunch of jurors around the courthouse."

Mark nodded. "I stand corrected. Besides, I'm sure it's a cool job for them because they get to hear everything that goes on." He hunched down and whispered. "Think about it. They hear not just what happens in the courtroom, but everything we say too."

"You really think they're listening to what happens in the jury room?" Brooke asked, wondering why it hadn't occurred to her and what she might have said that Leroy had overheard.

"I'm not saying they would spy on us, but I'm sure they can't help but hear things, right?"

He looked at Reggie as if seeking affirmation, but she merely shrugged. "They have better things to do than listen to people gripe about being called for jury duty. Like I said, they're in charge of security."

Mark seemed unfazed by Reggie's gruff demeanor. "Sure, but think about how much power they could have if they wanted to listen in. They could sway a verdict simply by telling the wrong person something they overheard."

Brooke shot a look at Reggie whose stare was boring holes through Mark's head. Meanwhile, Mark, seemingly oblivious, shoved a huge bite of his chicken fried steak into his mouth and hummed happily while gnawing at his meal. Brooke reached over and tapped Reggie's thigh under the table and Reggie nodded slightly and mouthed "not now."

Brooke raced through eating half of her meal and then pushed it aside, declaring it was great, but she was full. The truth was she was too jacked up to eat. All she wanted to do was get Reggie alone and discuss whether it was possible someone who worked at the courthouse, like god-forbid Leroy, was responsible for keeping tabs on her.

On the way out of the diner, Brooke stole a moment while Mark was loading up on mints by the cash register to have a brief whispered exchange with Reggie.

"Offer to drop us at the front of the courthouse," she said.

"But—"

"Trust me."

A few minutes later, Reggie pulled up to the courthouse steps. "No sense all of us walking from the garage," she said as she stopped her vehicle.

"Fine by me," Mark said, hopping out of the Jeep.

He reached back and held out a hand to Brooke, but she pretended to be fumbling for something in her purse. Finally, she looked up at him with a rueful expression. "Darn it, I really want my toothbrush, but I must've left it in my car. I'll grab it and walk back over with Reggie. See you in a few."

His smile faltered slightly, but he gave her a mock salute and walked away while Reggie drove toward the garage.

"He likes you."

Brooke shifted in her seat. "No, he doesn't. He's just socially awkward. Besides, he thinks you like me."

Reggie turned to look at her. "Maybe he's right. Maybe he's jealous."

Brooke felt the slow burn of a blush rise up her neck. "Maybe you're being silly."

"About what? That I like you or that he's jealous about it." She grinned. "Or both?"

Brooke laughed, partly relieved that the earlier tension between them had vanished and partly to mask the fact she wasn't sure what to do with this new information. She'd sensed Reggie had feelings for her, but to hear her say it out loud was another thing entirely. The standard cacophony of thoughts started in—the ones that always bubbled up whenever something in her personal life wrestled for attention. *There's no space in your life for another person. You barely have time for Ben. When he's older and you have your degree, you can have a life, but right now, you need to focus.*

That's right—stay the course, don't deviate. She'd worked hard her whole life and this week had been the first time her focus had been derailed. Some of it she couldn't control, like the jury summons and the threat from whoever, but she could control falling for a woman with whom she had nothing in common other than the brief circumstance of serving on a jury together.

Reggie parked her Jeep and took the keys out of the ignition. "Look," she said. "I didn't mean to put you on the spot. But after this is all over, if you'd like to go out sometime, I'd be up for that."

Cool, casual, and easy. All she had to say in response was, "sure," but Brooke couldn't manage to make even a fleeting promise. "Thanks. We should go or we're going to be late. Again."

"Okay."

Reggie jumped out of the Jeep. To any casual observer, she looked totally unfazed by the brush-off, but Brooke could see the tension back in her shoulders and a slight frown pulling at the corners of her eyes. She wanted to say something, but all she could think of was "it's not you, it's me," and someone like Reggie deserved more than a cliché. Instead she followed her in silence as they walked through the garage toward the courthouse. They hadn't walked far when suddenly Reggie grabbed her with both arms and shoved her behind a large cement pole. She placed a finger over her mouth, shook her head, and pointed a few feet away. Brooke followed her gaze and barely held back a gasp.

CHAPTER TWELVE

Reggie knew she shouldn't be surprised to see Harry Benton near the courthouse, but she could hardly believe he'd be caught dead in a parking garage. Men like him had drivers who got them as close to doors as possible, so they didn't have to mess up their hair or their clothes or mingle with the masses upon whom they'd built their fortunes. But more surprising than where he was, was who he was talking to—Shirley Mitchell—and their conversation didn't look particularly friendly.

She inched backward with Brooke in her arms, determined to stay out of sight, but desperately wanting to hear what these two Dallas power players were arguing about. She whispered in Brooke's ear, "Don't move."

"I won't."

Was she imagining Brooke pressing closer against her? She wasn't sure, but her body warmed to the touch, nearly threatening to distract her from what was happening a few feet away.

"What are you up to, Harry?"

"I have no idea what you're talking about." Benton smirked. "Don't you have a trial to get back to?"

"Don't you?"

"I'm not worried about my trial. It's going well. I've got a whole fleet of attorneys on my side. Could you only afford the one?"

"Gloria Leland is a bulldog. You should see her go after the state's witnesses."

"We'll see how she does when you're on trial for jury tampering."

Shirley's eyes narrowed. "What are you talking about?"

He laughed. "Don't try to play coy with me. I know you better than most. You and I are cut from the same cloth."

"That's what you'd have everyone believe, but I never needed to resort to threatening a judge to get my way. And what about your daughter, Harry? You know there's no statute of limitations for murder, right?"

"Don't act like you know things you don't, Shirley. The feds are on to you. You may skate on this trial, but they don't mess around. You keep your mouth shut and I'll take care of you. You have my word." He clasped her on the shoulder and his smile turned feral. "And if you talk? You have my word there will be consequences for someone you love. If you have any doubt, just ask the girl who we picked to be in charge of making sure you don't go to the pen."

Shirley merely stared at him with her mouth open, and Reggie didn't think there was any way she could be faking the shocked expression she wore. She looked down at Brooke and could tell she was thinking the same thing. How did Harry Benton know more about the threat on Brooke than the woman who stood the most to benefit?

"What have you done?" Shirley hissed the accusation.

"What I do best. Fix things. For you, for me. For all the people who depend on us to keep our business growing. I'm not going down, and if you stay in line, you won't either. Keep your mouth shut and let me handle the rest. If you decide to talk to the feds, all bets are off. Understood?"

Shirley didn't respond out loud, but Reggie thought she detected her head nodding in response to Benton's question. Before she could fully process what she'd just seen, Benton headed to the elevators and a few seconds later, Shirley took the catwalk back to the courthouse. When Brooke turned in her arms, Reggie snapped back into the moment.

"What the hell was that?" Brooke asked, her eyes brimming with indignation.

"Good question. Sounds like you're not the only one being threatened." Reggie looked around. More people were starting to enter the garage, probably because other courts were just now taking their lunch break. "We should get out of here."

Brooke eased out of her arms and backed a step away. Reggie stared into her eyes for a moment, wondering if she shared the empty feeling at the break of their embrace. Or was it just her, imagining an intimacy that was only present due to circumstance?

She shrugged the thought away. Brooke had made it clear she wasn't interested in her and she wasn't going to push the point. All that mattered right now was keeping Brooke safe, and to do that, she needed to find Sarah and Lennox to let them know about the exchange they'd just witnessed. "You go on. I'll find Lennox and tell her about this."

"I should come with you."

She wanted nothing more, but she needed a moment alone. "Nah, Leroy will lose it if we're both late. You go and I'll be there in a few."

Brooke looked like she wanted to say more, but she finally turned and headed to the catwalk. She was several steps away when she turned back. "Thank you. For everything."

Reggie didn't have a chance to respond before she walked away. Brooke's words were grateful and kind, but they fell like stones weighing down any feeling between them. Things were about to blow up in the courtroom and when it did, the trial would be over and so would the only thing that bound them together. All the things Reggie had wanted before she'd received the jury summons—peace in her life, freedom from this place, time to study—all faded in the background as she realized she'd never felt more alive than when she was helping, even on the fringe, root out an injustice by the side of a woman who made her feel things she'd relegated to the background of her life. The idea that tomorrow this might all be over, while a good thing for Brooke, left her feeling hollow and lonely.

She took a deep breath. Her feelings didn't matter right now. What mattered was making sure Benton went down and she needed to make sure that happened. She walked back to the courthouse, but instead of going to Judge Hunt's court, she went straight to Lennox's office. The door was open and she could see Sarah sitting across from her desk. Lennox waved her in, and she shut the door behind her.

"We need to talk."

❖

Brooke was still trying to process everything that had just happened, but she was distracted by the fact Reggie still wasn't back yet and Leroy looked like he was about to combust.

"She didn't say where she was going?"

"No." It was only a half lie since Reggie hadn't been specific about the where, only that she planned to talk to Lennox and she truthfully didn't know where Lennox's office was.

"Okay, I'll let the judge know, but he's not going to be happy."

Brooke wanted to say she wasn't happy either, but she merely nodded and walked to the other side of the room to stay out of the line of fire. She was pouring a cup of coffee she had no plans to drink when Mark appeared at her side.

"What happened?" he asked.

"Nothing." She didn't want to have this conversation and hoped he'd take the hint and walk away. No such luck.

"I mean she used to work here. You'd think she'd know the rules."

She whirled on him, ready to deliver a scathing speech about how he didn't know anything about Reggie and should keep his mouth shut, but she bit back the words when she realized she didn't really know anything about Reggie either.

Sure you do.

Her brain buzzed through a quick calculation of what she did know. Reggie was the kind of person who thought about other people's safety before her own. Who dropped what she was doing to help others out. Who took an interest in a stranger who was in distress. She was funny and kind. She knew plenty about Reggie, and Mark's implication grated on her nerves. "She had an important errand. I'm sure the judge will understand."

His eyes narrowed and for the first time Brooke wondered if his inquisitiveness was more than a byproduct of awkward social skills. Was *he* someone she should be cautious about? Could *he* be the someone that the ominous voice on the phone said had eyes on her?

She shook the thought away. Her fears were getting totally out of hand. Mark seemed harmless and her imagination caused her to spiral. "I'm sure if she's not here, she has a good reason."

At that moment, Reggie burst through the door to the jury room. She met Brooke's eyes, but quickly glanced away, walking over to the far side of the room and pouring herself a cup of coffee. Brooke watched her every move, willing her to look back again, come across the room, and pick up where they'd left off before she'd let things get weird between them. She'd explain to

Reggie that it had been so long since she'd dated, she'd forgotten how to even deal with the ask, but maybe when this trial was over, they could give it a go.

Right. A hot commodity like Reggie wasn't going to settle for snippets of time between her job, her studies, and a twelve-going-on-twenty-five-year-old son that consumed the balance of her free time. When thirty more minutes passed without Reggie even giving her a glance, her assessment was confirmed, and she resolved it was for the best.

"When do you think they're going to start back up?" Mark asked.

Brooke stared at him for a moment, having almost forgotten he was standing next to her, and then glanced up at the clock on the wall. The lunch break had ended over thirty minutes ago, and while it wasn't unusual for their breaks to last longer than the time the judge had ordered, Leroy had made it clear when he was asking about Reggie that the judge was raring to get started. "Good question."

A few minutes later, Leroy appeared in the doorway, his face red and flustered. "Judge is adjourning for the day. Plan to be back at nine a.m. tomorrow."

He remained in the doorway as the jurors filed out of the room. Brooke noticed Reggie didn't line up with the others, so she hung back, hoping to get a moment alone with her before they went their separate ways, but when the line began to dwindle and Reggie still hadn't moved, she started to the door only to have Leroy motion for her to stay put.

"The judge wants to see you both in chambers."

His words were gruff, but she couldn't tell if he was perturbed with them or the situation overall. Either way, it didn't look like she was going to get that alone time with Reggie anytime soon. She followed Leroy and Reggie followed her down the hallway behind the courtroom to an office with Judge Hunt's nameplate on the door. Leroy rapped on the door and announced them and then headed off in the opposite direction.

Judge Hunt rose from behind his desk and motioned for them to have a seat. "Sorry for the drama, but we need to talk to the two of you."

Brooke looked around for the "we," but didn't see anyone else in the room. As if he could read her mind, Judge Hunt pointed to the door where Leroy had returned escorting the prosecutor and defense attorney into the room, along with Agent Flores. Brooke tried to catch Reggie's eyes, but she was focused on the judge.

Once everyone was settled, Judge Hunt shook his head. "It seems we have a situation the likes of which I've never encountered before. Agent Flores, would you like to bring us up to speed?"

Sarah scooted to the edge of her seat. "Yes, Judge. We received a report from Ms. Knoll this afternoon that she overheard Harry Benton engaged in a heated conversation with Ms. Mitchell. Apparently, Ms. Dawson also heard this conversation, during which Mr. Benton implied that he was the one who'd orchestrated the attempted jury tampering previously reported by Ms. Dawson."

She turned and gestured to Gloria Leland. "Benton threatened Ms. Mitchell and her 'loved ones' with harm if she cooperated with law enforcement regarding the allegation of jury tampering or anything having to do with their shared business arrangements which may or may not be involved in the current charges against Ms. Mitchell."

Gloria rose from her chair. "My client has no reason to cooperate with the government because she not only didn't do anything wrong, but she doesn't know anything about these accusations."

"That's a lie."

Brooke immediately covered her mouth with her hand. She hadn't planned to say the words out loud, but it was too late to take them back now. She looked over at Reggie who gave her a hint of a smile which she took as encouragement to press on. "Harry Benton was in the parking garage this afternoon standing as close to Shirley Mitchell as I am to you now and he said 'I'm not going down, and if you stay in line, you won't either. Keep your mouth shut and let me handle the rest.'"

"You remember his exact words?" Gloria asked, her tone sarcastic.

"You would too if you'd received similar threats," Brooke retorted.

"Your Honor, *if* Harry Benton threatened my client and that's a big if, that doesn't make her culpable of any wrongdoing. But I will acknowledge that it seems like someone is certainly out to get Ms. Mitchell, and they will do anything, including trying to set her up for a crime she didn't commit, to take her down. I'd like to renew my motion for a mistrial."

Judge Hunt sighed and looked over at the prosecutor. "Mr. Rigley, do you have a response?"

"I don't know, Judge. It's clear the jury has been tampered with, but if you grant a mistrial, then the person who would've benefitted from the tampering is getting a pass."

"If your evidence is so great, you can simply retry the case," Leland shot back.

"You and I both know that retrials come with all sorts of issues—witness memory fades, witnesses disappear, evidence gets lost." Rigley shook his head. "I'm inclined to keep going."

"Not with a juror in the box who is predisposed to believe my client is guilty," Leland said.

"Didn't sound like she thought your client was guilty," Rigley retorted. "Sounded like she thought your client is a coward."

Hunt slammed his hand on the desk. "That's enough, both of you. Save your theatrics for the courtroom. Leroy, please escort Ms. Knoll and Ms. Dawson back to the jury room for now."

Brooke rose reluctantly from her seat. She wanted to know what was going to happen and she wanted to know now, but it wasn't like she could defy the judge and stick around. Nobody seemed to care that she was more exposed than ever now that Mitchell's attorney knew she'd heard Mitchell being threatened, not even Reggie. She'd wanted time alone with her, but now she wasn't so sure that was the best thing for either of them since Reggie seemed to care more about the outcome of this case than how it affected her.

CHAPTER THIRTEEN

Reggie followed Brooke into the jury room. She hadn't expected the judge to pull them into chambers, but if Mitchell was lying to her attorney about Benton's influence over her, it was probably for the best Leland had heard about it from someone who'd seen it all go down. Not that she'd believed it. Still, maybe there was a chance that, once they were alone, Leland would be able to convince her client she should take a deal and tell Flores how Benton had threatened her.

"What did you tell them?" Brooke asked.

Reggie kept her voice calm in response to the indignation in Brooke's voice. "I told Lennox and Sarah what we heard in the garage. That I think Benton is the one behind the threats against you and, if that's the case, they should beef up security on you and up surveillance on him."

"Did it ever occur to you I wouldn't want to be put on the spot like that? It's pretty clear, Mitchell's attorney thinks I'm a liar."

"Leland? That's just her personality. She's going to do or say whatever it takes to get the best deal for her client."

"It didn't sound like she wanted a deal at all. It sounded like she was only interested in getting all the charges dropped."

Reggie raised her hands in the air. "Why are you mad at me? What did you expect me to do?"

Brooke put her face in her hands. "I don't know. And I know I'm not sounding rational. I just want this whole thing to be over and I'm telling you, a mistrial sounds like the best thing in the world right about now."

Reggie looked around to make sure they were alone before stepping closer and pulling Brooke into her arms. "I get it. I really do, but if Benton is the one behind all of this, then I'm not sure a mistrial would end things. He'll think you went to the judge even though he or whoever is threatening you on his behalf told you not to."

"Did it ever occur to you he may think that anyway? How do you know Mitchell hasn't already told him?"

"If she did, she's a really good actress. Did she sound like she was mixed up in this when we heard them in the garage? She might be involved in some shady deals with him, but she sounded genuinely surprised when he brought up tampering with the jury."

Brooke sighed. "You're right." She eased out of Reggie's arms. "What do we do next?"

Reggie instantly missed the moment of intimacy and wanted to pull her back, but she resisted, knowing that with Brooke's life spinning out of control, anything between them had to be on her terms. "We wait and trust the process."

"Not an easy thing to do."

Reggie smiled. "I know, but I'm right here if you need me. You don't have to go through this alone."

Brooke reached for her hand and threaded her fingers through hers. "Thank you."

They stared at each other for a moment, while Reggie ran through a list of lines she wanted to say, but before she could settle on one, the sound of the door opening startled them both and Brooke stepped back, dropping her hand in the process.

Leroy poked his head in the door. "Judge says you can go. Asked me to remind you not to talk to anyone about what happened in chambers. Got it?"

"Got it," Reggie answered for both of them. When he shut the door, she pulled out her keys. "Let me save you an Uber and drive you home?"

"Only if you let me make dinner. It's going to be omelets this time, though. I haven't exactly had time to grocery shop."

Reggie hesitated for a moment knowing she should take advantage of the early release to study, but torn by the prospect of some alone time with Brooke.

"It's okay if you have other plans," Brooke said, her tone wistful.

"My other plans consist of flash cards for the PI exam."

"I'm excellent with flash cards. Besides, Ben needs to study and so do I. We could have a study date."

Reggie latched onto the word date and made her decision. "Well, I do love a good omelet."

Brooke laughed. "I didn't say it would be good."

Reggie reached for her hand and led her to the door. She had no idea where a study date might lead, but she was up for just about anything that included her and Brooke—far away from the courthouse and this case.

CHAPTER FOURTEEN

B rooke opened the front door, hoping Ben hadn't left a mess in the living room. Yes, Reggie had already been over once, but that time she'd just cleaned the house and known it hadn't been a wreck before she invited Reggie in. Since then, her life had spiraled out of control, and keeping the house clean seemed like a bridge too far.

"Everything okay?" Reggie asked.

Brooke stepped aside, deciding to surrender to whatever mess might greet them on the other side of the door. "Don't judge me by the way my place looks."

"No judgment here. My apartment looks like a college freshman has been bingeing for exams. Lots of empty take-out food containers and Post-it notes on every surface."

"And here I thought you were an index card kind of woman."

"I'm full of surprises."

Reggie winked and Brooke warmed to the flirting, her resolve to keep her distance melting away. Who was she kidding? She'd invited Reggie for dinner, and it wasn't simply to thank her for serving as her private transport. She wanted to spend time with her, away from the courthouse and all the chaos of the trial. Reggie was the first person she'd been attracted to that she'd introduced to her son in years, and even if the introduction was the result of accidental circumstance, she had no regrets.

She led the way to the kitchen and pointed at the small table. "We have a rule in this house that we have to at least start our homework before dinner, so break out the books, Miss Private Eye."

"Seems like a fair rule," Reggie said, sliding into one of the chairs. "What about you?"

Brooke gestured to a backpack hanging over the back of one of the chairs. "Believe it or not, that's mine. Yes, I carry a backpack. Unlike my spoiled middle-schooler, we don't have lockers at Richards University."

"Actually, I was referring to your title. I mean, I know you're going to school, but what's the end game?"

"Are you asking me what I want to be when I grow up?"

"I'm not an advocate of the growing up part, but at the risk of sounding corny, what's your major?"

"Great question. I'm still working on that one. Right now, I'm working on getting the basics out of the way. I'm leaning toward a business degree, but I have a passion for liberal arts, and I've thought about teaching." She shrugged. "Then some days I wonder why I even bother. By the time I finish whatever degree I decide on, there'll be a bunch of other, much younger job candidates lined up to take the first spots."

"Life experience beats youth every day of the week."

Brooke smiled. "Remember that when I apply for the job of running your very successful PI business."

"I will."

Brooke stared into Reggie's eyes, looking for something, anything, to signal this woman was too good to be true. She was beautiful and sweet and chivalrous and smart. She was great with Ben and didn't seem to mind eating sandwiches or omelets or doing homework around a tiny kitchen table. All her observations led to one solitary thought, and she blurted it out before she could stop herself. "Why are you single?"

Reggie looked shocked at first and then she burst into laughter. "Why are you?"

"You first," Brooke said, determined to get an answer now that she'd gone down this path.

"I don't know. I've dated plenty, but I guess I haven't found the right person." She touched her shoulder. "After the shooting, I decided to focus on myself. I quit my job and applied for my license and then there wasn't any extra time for meeting new people."

"Yet here we are."

"Yes."

The air was heavy with the words they weren't saying until Brooke finally felt compelled to break the silence. "I'm glad you're here."

"Me too."

"And I'm sorry I resisted at first." Brooke waved her arm in a circle. "This can be a lot for some folks. Built-in family and all."

"I get it. And you probably don't introduce your son to new people right off the bat."

"Definitely not in hospital emergency rooms," Brooke said with a grin. "You must be some kind of special."

Reggie stood and walked to her side. "I don't know about that, but I definitely think you are."

"Add charming to the list." Brooke's breath quickened as Reggie drew closer and whispered in her ear.

"You think I'm charming?"

"Among other things."

"As much as I'd love to hear more, I'd rather kiss you." Reggie leaned back slightly and looked directly in her eyes. "If that's okay."

"If you don't, I'm going to come out of my skin."

Brooke barely got the words out before Reggie's lips were on hers. Soft, yet firm, she kissed her slowly at first—light, tender touches, each carrying the promise of more. Brooke kissed her back and their pace quickened. She was hungry for Reggie's touch and opened her mouth, inviting her in. Reggie's tongue met hers and she melted against the touch.

Somewhere in the distance a buzzing sound edged into her consciousness, and she brushed at the air with her hand as if swatting away a fly, but the noise continued until she couldn't ignore it any longer. Reluctantly, she eased out of Reggie's embrace. "Do you hear that?"

Reggie's eyes were hooded and dark and her lips were swollen. "What?" She looked around. "Oh, wait. It's your phone." She pointed at the table. "It's buzzing."

Brooke jerked out of her own haze when she saw Ben's picture on the screen. She grabbed the phone. "Ben, are you okay?"

"Sure, but have you seen the news?"

"What?" She couldn't compute why her twelve-year-old son was asking her about the news and it wasn't just because she was high from Reggie's kiss. "What's going on?"

"I just texted you the link. Isn't that the lady whose trial you're on?"

Brooke punched the button to put her phone on speaker and laid it on the table while she scrolled through her texts. Ben had sent her a link to a live newsfeed with a reporter on the scene at Shirley Mitchell's house in Highland Park. Brooke couldn't tell at first what was going on, but after she read the caption at the top of the screen, she knew she wanted Ben home. Right now. She spoke carefully, so as not to alarm him. "Thanks, Ben. You better get on home. It's time for dinner."

"Okay, Mom," he said, disconnecting the line.

"What is it?" Reggie asked.

Brooke pointed at the screen and turned up the volume.

"Returning live to our reporter in the field, Bruce Tasco who is at the home of Shirley Mitchell, the developer currently on trial

for fraud. An intruder broke into her home earlier this evening. Bruce, what can you tell us so far?"

"Not much, Suzanne. A neighbor called in the report and, although the Mitchell residence has a registered security system, the intruder would have eluded detection if the next-door neighbor hadn't happened to see him from their upstairs window."

"Were the police able to apprehend the suspect?"

"According to my sources, the intruder escaped, but the police cordoned off the house and called for a crime scene unit." The camera panned to the street and zoomed in on a CSU van. *"It's my understanding Mitchell wasn't home at the time, but her children were here with their nanny, although I do not know if they were in the area of the house where the intruder broke in."*

"Any word on a motive or if this break-in has anything to do with the pending trial?"

"That remains to be seen. I've spoken with several neighbors and shock is the common thread of their responses. Break-ins aren't common in this neighborhood, and the general feeling is this has to be an anomaly."

"Thanks, Bruce. We'll come back to you later to see if there are any updates."

Brooke closed the app and checked her texts. Nothing. She checked the time. Ben had stayed after school to do some extra credit work with Mr. Lawrence who'd promised to drop him at home when they were done. School was a five-minute drive from here. If they'd gotten in the car right after she'd talked to Ben, they should be pulling up to the house right about now.

"Brooke?"

She jerked around, half surprised to see Reggie still standing there. "Sorry, stuck in my head."

"Ben's going to be okay."

"He should be home now."

Reggie pointed at the phone. "We don't know if that has anything to do with Harry Benton."

"Come on, Reggie, you know we do. Do you think it's a coincidence that someone tried to break into Shirley Mitchell's house the same day that Benton threatened her? You of all people should know what he is capable of."

Reggie flinched slightly at the comment and Brooke regretted going there, but she stood by her point. "I do. That's why I made sure Ben has an officer watching out for him."

Brooke stepped closer and put her arms around Reggie, leaning her forward against hers. "I'm sorry. That was a shitty thing to say."

Reggie tightened their embrace. "You're worried. I get it. You have every right to be and I'm right there with you."

The creak of the front door opening caused them both to turn in that direction. Brooke slipped out of Reggie's arms and raced to the door to find Ben shrugging out of his backpack.

"Hi, Mom. Did you watch the video?"

She wrapped him in her arms, ignoring his plea that she was squeezing him too tight. "I did. What made you think to send it to me?"

"I dunno. I recognized the name. If someone broke into her house, is someone going to break into ours because you're involved in the trial?" He looked over her shoulder. "Hi, Reggie! Are you staying for dinner?"

"Hi, Ben." Reggie looked directly at her and cocked her head as if she thought the invitation might be revoked. When Brooke didn't respond, she said, "Not sure about dinner yet, but if not tonight, maybe some other time."

Brooke turned his words over in her head while he regaled Reggie with stories about his day. Despite not knowing about the threat on his own life, he'd connected the trial with danger and why shouldn't he? She should be the one protecting him, not some random cop that didn't even know him. Yet, here she was, standing in the kitchen kissing Reggie like she didn't have a care in the world. She needed to get her head straight and that meant no more distractions. And Reggie Knoll was a huge distraction.

"Ben, go clean up for dinner and let me talk to Reggie for a minute."

He groaned at the words "clean up," but scampered out of the room, telling Reggie he'd be right back. She stared after him for a moment before turning back to Reggie.

"I should go."

Despite the declaration, Reggie stayed in place and this was the perfect opportunity to tell her no, she should stay, but as much as she wanted to be back in Reggie's arms, giving in to her own desires felt like a betrayal of her parental duties. "I'm sorry."

Reggie placed a finger under her chin and tilted it up toward her. "You have to stop staying that. You have nothing to be sorry for."

"It's bad timing."

"I get it."

"I wish it weren't, if that makes it any easier."

Reggie glanced away. "Easy is overrated." She turned to go, but paused with her hand on the door. "You deserve all the things, Brooke. I hope that someday you realize that and give yourself permission to have them."

She watched as Reggie walked away, wishing she had the courage to call her back. But her life was already full of things she could barely handle and a woman who could turn her to Jell-O with one kiss would only divert her focus. She was doing the right thing. She was sure.

Mostly.

CHAPTER FIFTEEN

Reggie walked out of the jury room, thankful they'd adjourned early for the day and determined to get as far away from the other jurors as possible. She'd managed to avoid Brooke all day, which was hard to do in the small jury room with only eleven other people—a mission made easier by Brooke's apparent desire to steer clear of her as well. What she really wanted was for this trial to be over, but Judge Hunt had made his decision—they were going to press on as if nothing had happened.

Mark Landon had sidled up to her at one point to ask if everything was okay between her and Brooke, and she barely resisted the desire to punch him in the face. Apparently, she'd used up all of her cool last night at Brooke's place when she'd pretended she didn't care about the out-of-the-blue brush-off right on the heels of the amazing kiss they'd shared.

She tried to tell herself she shouldn't care. A week ago, she'd been single and happy about it, content to focus on her new career and determined not to let anything get in the way of her new path. But meeting Brooke had changed all that, and now she could hardly focus on anything else. She'd wound up ditching her damn flash cards for a couple of beers after she'd left Brooke's place, which only made things worse.

She walked down the hall to the courtroom where Harry Benton's trial was still in full swing, but she was only halfway there when Skye Keaton called out to her.

"Hey," Skye said. "Lennox is looking for you."

"It's not like I'm hard to find. I'm stuck on a jury, pretending that this process means something."

Skye frowned. "Not following."

Reggie glanced around to make sure no one was listening to their conversation. "I'm sure you heard about the break-in at Shirley Mitchell's house last night."

"I did. She lives down the street from us."

Reggie narrowed her eyes. "You must do really well in the private eye game."

Skye laughed. "I do okay, but my wife's the one who makes the big bucks. We live in Highland Park because that's where most of her real estate clients are, not because I'm footing the bill."

"Well, we're in trial acting like nothing's wrong, but meanwhile, I'm certain Harry Benton has threatened Mitchell and that's what the break-in was about," Reggie said. "I don't get it. Why this trial is still happening since any good attorney will be able to figure out how to get it tossed on appeal."

Skye rolled her eyes. "Come with me."

Reggie followed her, silently grousing as they rode the elevator to the tenth floor. She was being shut out on so many levels, first with Brooke and now with her pals at the courthouse. Whatever this was about, it better involve some answers.

When they turned left out of the elevators toward the public defender's office, she hung back for a moment. "What's up?"

"Your presence has been requested. I hope you like coffee." Skye nodded to the receptionist and led the way behind the counter to the suite of offices used by the PD. She stopped a few feet in and rapped on one of the doors. Two quick knocks followed by two slower ones.

Reggie stepped back. "Seriously, Skye. What's with the spy knock?"

"Trust me."

The door opened and Lennox's girlfriend, Wren, was standing on the other side. She motioned for them to join her inside where Lennox and Sarah were seated around her desk. "I'm pretty sure we decided on three quick knocks followed by two slow ones," she said to Skye.

"Then why did you open the door?" Skye asked.

"Because I'm also pretty sure no one in this building is trying to decode your secret knock to get into my office."

"They might if they knew what you were brewing in here."

Reggie cleared her throat. "Would someone mind telling me what the hell is going on?"

Wren pointed at an empty chair. "Have a seat. Do you take cream and sugar with your coffee?"

She fought the urge to scream. Coffee service wasn't even close to the first thing on her mind right now, but Wren was staring at her intently, waiting for her response, so she decided to play along for now. "Cream, no sugar."

"Good choice." Wren reached for a mug on the shelf behind her desk and poured from a French press. She added a splash of creamer and stirred it in with an expensive-looking silver spoon. When Reggie took the mug from her outstretched hand, Wren motioned for her to try it, so she dutifully complied. The brew was smooth and rich, and for a brief moment, she focused solely on the moment.

"It's good, right?" Skye said.

"It's probably the best coffee I've ever had," Reggie said.

"I heard a 'but' on the end of that compliment," Wren said.

Reggie sighed. "Yep. How about this—*but* as much as I'm enjoying this coffee, I'm still wondering what I'm doing here."

"Plotting, of course." Wren motioned to the rest of the group. "We do our best plotting right here and we're inviting you to be a part of it. It has to be secret because you're on a jury right now and Lennox and Sarah shouldn't be telling you what they're about to tell you."

Reggie wanted to know how a PI, a PD, an ADA, and an FBI agent had all wound up plotting together, but more than that, she wanted to know what they had to tell her, so she simply nodded.

Sarah shoved an envelope across the desk at her. "Take a look at this."

Reggie folded back the flap and slid the note out of the envelope and instantly recoiled. The mismatched tape and glue letters formed an ominous message: *Cooperate and die.* The message was simple, to the point, and delivered in the form of haphazardly placed letters cut from a magazine. She dropped the note on the table. "Where did you get this?"

"It turned up at Shirley Mitchell's house after the intruder was there last night."

Reggie thought back to the conversation she'd witnessed in the parking garage between Shirley and Harry Benton. "She must've been pretty spooked to share it with you."

"She didn't and I'm not sure she ever would've, but one of her kids found the note and gave it to the nanny," Sarah said. "Nanny called the cops who should've found the note when they were there to investigate the break-in."

Reggie stared at the note a moment longer. "It sure looks like the ones Brooke's received."

"Exactly."

"You think Harry Benton is leaving threatening notes around town?"

"I think he's having it done."

It tracked. And she could understand why Benton might be sending notes threatening to harm Shirley Mitchell, but why would he also be sending notes to a juror on Mitchell's trial that were designed to help her? Unless...

"He's desperate for her to be found not guilty." Her thoughts churned faster now. "He's scared if she's found guilty or thinks the trial is going south, she might offer up some of the inside information she has on him for a plea or at sentencing in a last-ditch effort to avoid prison time. So, he set up this plan—tamper with the jury to change the outcome."

"Which might have worked had you not told us about what happened to Brooke's son," Lennox chimed in. "Once Judge Hunt knew about the threats against Brooke, they were no longer effective, so Benton stopped threatening Brooke and risked going straight to the source."

"Okay, but how did Benton find out the judge knew?" Reggie asked. "I thought Judge Hunt had a meeting in chambers with just the attorneys and Sarah."

"Any one of them could've talked."

"Johnny Rigley is one of my best prosecutors," growled Lennox. "He didn't talk."

"Can't say the same about Gloria Leland though, can you?" Wren asked.

"True."

Reggie rapped on the table to get everyone's attention. "Let me get this straight. What you're saying is that when Benton figured out threatening Brooke wasn't going to work anymore, he decided to frame Mitchell for jury tampering which isn't that hard considering he's the one who has all the evidence since he arranged the whole scheme."

"Exactly," Lennox said.

"I guess that would make it less likely anyone would believe anything she had to say if she then tried to flip on Benton." Reggie started to wrap her mind around the idea. "She'd only look like she was desperate to avoid prison time." She looked around the room. "So, what do we do know?"

"I think it's time we bring Mitchell back in," Sarah said. "Now that her own family has been targeted with threats, she might be more willing to talk."

Reggie flashed back to the conversation between Benton and Mitchell in the parking garage. "I don't know if that will be enough. Based on what I saw, those two have a really disturbing dynamic. They might take each other down, but I doubt either one of them would want to involve law enforcement to do it." An idea started to churn in the back of her mind, but it was too crazy to say out loud.

"What are you thinking?" Lennox asked. She rolled her hand in the air. "Out with it."

Reggie faced the intense gaze of the others in the room. Yeah, her idea might be crazy, but she was in a safe space here. "Mitchell knows I overheard her conversation with Benton, but what if she thought I knew even more?"

Sarah looked skeptical. "Like what?"

"Like what if there was another note—just like the others, and another juror being coerced to vote not guilty? At some point, when the evidence starts to pile up, it becomes undeniable. Maybe then she can be convinced there's no way out for her other than to give up whatever she's got on Harry Benton."

"And this other juror is you, right?"

"Yes, but let's do things differently this time. Instead of her attorney getting hauled into chambers and her getting threatened with legal action, what if I try and coerce her into telling me about Benton's involvement in the shooting in exchange for my silence?"

"You said yourself, they have a strange dynamic," Lennox said. "She's not going to rat Benton out to you."

"I said it was strange, but it's not perfect. She would love nothing more than to put Benton away, but she's not going to come clean with you people—why would she trust the DA's office when you indicted her?

"And you, Sarah, she's never going to implicate herself in a conspiracy when everyone knows all the bad actors are going to do time, it's just a matter of how much. But I can appeal to her not only as someone who can shore up the tampering case, but also a victim of Benton's atrocities." She rubbed her injured arm to emphasize the point.

Skye was the first to speak. "She has a point."

"And if Mitchell goes running to Benton and asks for his help to get rid of the problem?" Sarah shook her head. "It's dangerous. We need a more controlled plan."

"Sarah, you're great," Lennox said, "But you've got to lose the fed mentality. Sometimes you have to go rogue to get stuff done." She turned to Reggie. "If you get caught talking to Mitchell, the plan falls apart. Are you sure you're up for this?"

Reggie paused for only a second, knowing if she took too long to respond, her answer might change. But in that flicker of time, she thought of Brooke and Ben, and she knew she had to do something to end this once and for all. "A hundred percent."

Chapter Sixteen

B rooke tried her best to appear casual as she walked up and down the hall outside of Judge Hunt's courtroom, but she could tell by some of the looks she was drawing that she looked more lost than nonchalant.

Accurate. She was lost and she'd been that way since last night when Reggie had delivered the most incredible kiss she'd ever had in her life. Strike that. She'd been anything but lost in the throes of the kiss, but afterward when Reggie left her house, she'd never felt more alone, and the feeling persisted still.

Reggie had barely looked at her all morning, exchanging only a quick hello before burying her head in a book, studying no doubt, which was another painful reminder of last night's abrupt ending. Not for the first time, Brooke wondered what was wrong with her that she couldn't let someone like Reggie get close. Ben liked her and, based on what she'd seen, so did everyone here at the courthouse. Reggie had done nothing but be kind and helpful to her and all she'd done was push her away.

"Where's your friend?"

Brooke turned to see Mark standing directly behind her, a little closer than she preferred, but she wrote it off to his social awkwardness. "Hi, Mark. Are you as tired as I am of sitting?" She hoped he wouldn't notice she hadn't answered his question.

"I saw her earlier, but then she disappeared."

Brooke sighed. "I'm sure she had some things to do on the break."

"Wanna get some lunch?"

She hadn't planned to, partly because she had no appetite despite skipping dinner the night before, and partly because she'd hoped to run into Reggie if she continued to pace the hallway. Both reasons were dumb. She would never make it through the afternoon if she didn't eat, and wherever Reggie was, she wasn't interested in joining her. Mark wasn't the company she wanted, but listening to him jabber was better than playing back all the stewing thoughts in her head. "Sure."

A few minutes later, they were in Mark's car headed down Riverside Drive. While Mark focused on the road, Brooke looked around the car and rubbed her hand on the supple leather interior of the BMW. "Nice car," she said.

He glanced over and smiled like he was proud of himself, but all he said was "thanks."

Brooke fished around for something to talk about, but she wasn't interested in small talk, so when Mark brought up the trial, she didn't try to steer him away from the subject.

"Do you think Shirley's going to take the stand?"

She hesitated, leery about whether this was some kind of ethics test, but eventually she gave in to the desire to break down their experience. "Good question. What do you think?"

"I kind of think she will. She's a tough person, but she's not going to like the fact all these people are trying to make her out to be some kind of weakling who has to pay people off to get her way."

Brooke replayed his words in her head, trying to figure out what he'd said that bothered her, but she couldn't quite put her finger on it. "I know we're not supposed to talk about the case, but I'm finding it fascinating how many contractors think they have to pay off city officials to get anything done. I'm not sure I'd last long in their line of business."

"It's the way deals are done," he said as if it was nothing. "Might not be how I prefer it, but if everyone's on board, what's the harm?" He pulled into the parking lot in front of a row of food trucks and stopped the car.

She stared at him and he stared back. "What's the matter?" he asked.

"You don't really believe that, do you?"

"It's no different than consensual sex."

"Okay, now you've lost me."

"Two people doing whatever they want to be happy—might involve some play that I wouldn't find appealing but doesn't matter if it's not me doing the deed."

And he'd suddenly made the whole thing sound even more sordid. "Yeah, not making the connection there. What two people choose to do in the privacy of their home is a lot different than conspiring to break the law."

"I guess so." He pointed to the food truck. "You hungry?"

She wasn't really, and hadn't been since last night, but it seemed weird to say so now that they were here. "I could eat something."

They ordered sliders and Mark insisted on paying despite her initial resistance. Truthfully, she was grateful not to have to shell out for lunch, considering she was feeling the pain of not working this week. She'd hoped after the break-in at Shirley Mitchell's house last night that the trial might get delayed or canceled altogether, allowing her to pick up some shifts, but apparently nothing was going to derail the proceeding.

They picked up their food and sat at one of the picnic tables by the truck. Mark tucked into his meal with gusto, but Brooke's first bite tasted like sandpaper and she nibbled around the edges to be polite.

After a few minutes of awkward small talk, Mark said, "I don't think she's guilty."

Brooke stared at him for a moment, watching him wipe his fingers carefully on a napkin and feeling a bit like she was being tested. "Is that right?"

"Yes. The people who've testified against her all carry grudges for one reason or another. Seems to me like they all decided to make her the target to avoid being in trouble themselves."

"So, you think she didn't do anything wrong, and she's being set up?" Brooke fought hard to keep her tone neutral. She shouldn't be letting herself get sucked into this situation in the first place, but now that it was happening, she needed to watch what she said.

"Of course. Isn't it perfectly clear?"

"I don't think anything is perfectly clear," she responded, keeping her voice low. "Besides, we won't be making any decisions until after we've heard all of the evidence and discussed the case as a group."

He smirked. "Right. Got it." He placed a finger over his lips. "The case will be decided by a jury of Shirley Mitchell's peers after careful deliberation."

He rolled his eyes as he spoke, and the singsong lilt of his voice set off alarm bells in Brooke's head. What had seemed like garden variety social awkwardness now came off a bit more sinister, and she was ready to be back at the courthouse with a crowd of people to serve as a buffer. She opened her mouth to say she was ready to go, but Mark's phone rang and, after glancing quickly at the screen, he stepped away to take the call.

While he was gone, Brooke looked at her own phone, half expecting a missed call or at least a text from Reggie, but there were no messages of any kind. It was silly of her to expect Reggie to reach out when she'd been the one who'd pushed her away, but she couldn't help but wish she'd pushed for a pause instead of a full on break between them.

"We need to go," Mark said. He gave his phone a final look and shoved it into his pocket.

She shoved aside her plate of barely eaten food, too grateful to be heading back to the courthouse to ask why he was in such a hurry all of a sudden. Maybe once they got back, she'd find a moment to have a word with Reggie, explain away her actions, and ask for a chance to start again when this trial was over.

She was so lost in thought about what she'd say to Reggie when she saw her that she didn't notice they were headed in the wrong direction until they were almost to Oak Cliff. She glanced over at Mark who was hunched over the wheel, staring intently at the road ahead. "Uh, where are we going?"

"I forgot something at my place. I just need to run in real quick. It'll only take a minute."

That explained why he'd been in such a rush to abandon lunch, but the change in plans left Brooke feeling on edge. She started to pull out her phone and send a text to Reggie, but stopped when Mark pulled into a driveway in front of a yellow bungalow house with beautiful, well-tended garden beds. Convinced she was agitated over nothing, she relaxed as he exited the car and closed her eyes for a moment to fantasize about changing her life once this trial was over. She needed to switch to night classes only, online where possible, and tell her boss she needed a regular schedule instead of switching from days to nights from week to week. She needed to spend more quality time with Ben and she needed to find time for her own needs, starting with exploring her feelings for Reggie. She was laser-focused on her newfound determination when her door jerked open and a hand, rough and hard, covered her mouth. Her eyes shot open and the last thing she saw before she faded into unconsciousness was Mark standing over her, smirking once again.

❖

When the judge recessed for the lunch break, Reggie dodged the other jurors on her way out of the jury room, determined to get to where she knew Mitchell's car was parked as quickly as possible. She ducked into the restroom in the basement of the courthouse, retrieved a ball cap from her jacket pocket, and tugged it low over her forehead before she dashed out of the building. She found Mitchell's driver exactly where Sarah said he would be—on the opposite of the courthouse from where all the regular folks entered. Typical.

She glanced around and, convinced no one was watching, she strode right up to the door of the car and rapped on the passenger side window. The driver lowered the window and glared when he saw it wasn't the person he was expecting, but she reached in and opened the door before he could raise the window.

"What do you think you're doing?"

She ignored him and slid into the seat next to him and placed her hand on his as he reached for his phone. "Don't. I need to speak to your boss and it's urgent. Trust me, she's going to want to hear what I have to say."

He wasn't falling for it. She could tell by the pucker of his mouth and the way he narrowed his eyes, but at that moment, the back door opened, and Mitchell slid into the seat behind her apparently not noticing there was an extra passenger up front.

"I'm starving, Elgon. You know any place that can serve a steak in less than an hour?"

Reggie turned and leaned over the back of the seat. "What about the jurors who are getting paid a measly forty bucks a day to decide your fate? Are you going to let them eat steak too?"

It only took a second for Mitchell to recognize her, but Reggie didn't wait for her to speak. "Tell Elgon to start driving. You and I need to have a conversation."

Mitchell nodded at Elgon who was staring at her in the rearview mirror and he pulled away from the curb. "Drive us someplace where we can talk in private," Reggie commanded, injecting her voice with more authority than she felt at that moment.

At Mitchell's nod, he drove across the Commerce Bridge, toward Oak Cliff and, at Mitchell's instruction, pulled off the road near the Trinity River Park—an unlikely place to run into fellow jurors or courthouse personnel on their lunch break. When he parked the car, Mitchell told him to get out and leave them alone.

"Are you that abrupt with all of your employees?" Reggie asked, genuinely wanting to know the answer.

"I'm whatever I have to be to get things done."

"Good to know." She turned in her seat, trying to find a comfortable position where she could face Mitchell and look like she was in control of the situation. "How about you and I take a little walk outside?"

"How about you fuck off? I don't know what you think you're doing, but whatever it is, it's not appropriate for us to be seen together."

"Right," Reggie said a little taken aback by the outburst from Mitchell who usually appeared to have a calm demeanor. "Because you only threaten jurors, not hang out with them."

"I never threatened anyone."

"I know." Reggie watched Mitchell's indignant expression turn curious. "I know it's Harry Benton who's forcing your hand, but if these keep showing up during your trial, no one else is going to believe that." She brandished the note she'd been carrying around in her pocket all morning—the copy Wren had made for her using the specifics Sarah had provided from the real ones that were in the FBI evidence locker. Mitchell flinched at the sight of the note.

"I had nothing to do with that."

"Like I said, no one is going to believe that you don't have anything to do with these notes that keep popping up. You're the only one that benefits from jurors being threatened to vote not guilty. Unless…"

A moment passed and Mitchell's anxiety was palpable. "Unless what?" she finally blurted out.

"Unless someone is trying to set you up or make it so you keep your mouth shut about something bigger than your case—something someone might kill for to keep quiet."

Mitchell laughed, but the sound was more nervous than mirthful. "You're crazy."

"I'm not." Reggie stared hard at Mitchell, enjoying the way she struggled not to squirm. "I heard him threaten you in the parking garage. He's got big secrets to hide and I bet you know exactly what those are. I bet you know more about his involvement in the shooting at the courthouse and he'll do anything to keep you quiet." She held up the note again. "If delivering you a not guilty doesn't work to ensure your silence, he may decide it's best to keep you quiet another way. A more permanent method."

"You really think Harry Benton would kill me because he's afraid I'll tell the police what I know?"

Reggie tried to raise her left arm and winced at the pain that lingered still. "See that?" she asked, pointing to her shoulder. "I can't lift my arm because a bullet went through it. I know in my heart Harry Benton was behind the shooting, but I bet you know it for a fact which is why he's working so hard to help you out."

"Even if I did know anything, why would I tell you about it?"

"Because we're both in the same boat—being threatened by a man with no scruples or sense of loyalty. The moment he thinks you're not on his side, he's going to take you down. But if you tell me what you know, I can do your dirty work for you.

He never has to know you were involved." She paused. "Let me have this justice. He practically ruined my life."

Mitchell stared at her for a moment, and Reggie was just starting to think she'd gotten through to her when Mitchell said, "I have no idea what you're talking about and I need you to get out of my car." She pointed at the door. "Right now."

Reggie shook her head but did as she was told and climbed out of the car. Elgon, who was standing sentry a few feet away passed her on his way back to the car. "Have fun," Reggie said as he walked by.

She watched as the car drove away and then she pulled out her phone and ordered a ride. While she waited, she called Lennox who answered on the first ring.

"How did it go?"

"About how we expected."

"Did you get everything done?"

"I did."

"Now we wait," Lennox said. "Where are you?"

"Trinity River Park. I called for an Uber. Be back in a few."

Reggie disconnected the call and spent the time waiting, wondering what Brooke was doing right now. Was she having lunch with Lisa and Jenny or was she taking time on the break to study? When this was all over, would she reconsider her desire not to get involved with her or would they never see each again?

She shook her head. Whatever Brooke decided, she had no control over it. All she could do was make sure Brooke was safe from the likes of Harry Benton and that Benton went away for a long time for the things he'd done.

CHAPTER SEVENTEEN

T hey are going to wonder where we are," Brooke said, trying to keep her voice calm. She was groggy from whatever Mark had used to drug her, which helped her keep her composure, but it also made it hard for her to think her way out of her predicament.

"Only you. I'll be back at the courthouse in a flash," Mark said as he fastened her hands together with zip ties. He stepped back to examine his work while she tried without success to see something, anything, but the blindfold covering her eyes was firmly fixed in place. She smelled something vaguely familiar, lavender maybe, but other than that she didn't have a clue as to her location.

"What's your plan?" she asked, half hoping he was egotistical enough to brag about what he was up to. Her bet paid off.

"You didn't get the hints I gave you about what to do on the jury, so I decided a little mistrial is in order." He paused for a moment and then the singsong voice was back. "It was so odd. Juror number twelve went to lunch and never came back. I've never heard of anything like it."

She grew cold at his laugh and quietly wrestled against her bonds while she struggled to come up with something to say to get out of this situation. "Wait, there's an alternate. If I don't show up, they'll just substitute him in for me. The trial will go on and there's nothing you can do to stop it."

He laughed again. "Nope. Mr. Alternate has dropped out. Word is he met the same fate as dear old Mr. Rodriguez."

Brooke swallowed a gasp as she remembered Rodriguez, the juror whose dramatic collapse in the courtroom had sealed her fate as one of the twelve. Whoever was behind the attempt to rig this trial had enormous reach. Much bigger than she or even Reggie had anticipated.

Thinking of Reggie caused her to wonder what she was doing right now. Was she at the courthouse, finishing up a sandwich at the cafeteria in the basement or was she with her friends who worked there, sharing a meal, maybe even laughing about the woman who couldn't even commit to a simple date?

No, Reggie wasn't the kind of person to kiss and tell or make fun. Reggie was kind and loyal. She'd pushed Reggie away for no good reason. If she got out of her current situation alive, she vowed to make it right, which made her even more determined to escape whatever this was. "Are you seriously going to keep me here until the trial is over?"

His laugh sounded patronizing this time and before he could answer, her mind filled in the blanks. She knew who'd abducted her and knew his motive. He wasn't just going to keep her here until the trial was over—he couldn't risk leaving her alive.

But if that was the case, why didn't he simply kill her now and get it over with? Maybe, there was someone else charged with doing the real dirty work and Mark was merely a cog in the machine of Benton's evil enterprise.

As if in answer to her question, Mark gagged her. "I have to go since two missing jurors would be super suspicious. Don't worry, someone will be by to look in on you soon. It was nice knowing you, Brooke."

She heard his footsteps and the sound of the door closing. She counted to thirty before struggling against her bonds, full force, but she succeeded in doing nothing more than cutting her wrists against the hard plastic of the zip ties. She screamed, but only muffled sounds emerged, and it was unlikely any neighbors were home in the middle of the day to hear her distress. After a few minutes of sustained effort, she took a deep breath and considered her plight. She was stuck here until help came or she came up with a solid idea for escape, and all she could hope was that Ben was okay, and that when she didn't turn up at the courthouse, someone, hopefully Reggie, would realize that she wasn't flaking out, but was in real danger. After what seemed like forever, despair settled in with the lingering effects of whatever drug Mark had used, and against her will, her eyes fluttered closed and she surrendered to a dream of Reggie bursting through the door to save the day.

❖

Reggie pushed through the door and walked down the hall behind the courtroom, ignoring the instructions about staying in the jury room. Brooke wasn't back from lunch and no one professed to have seen her during the break. Mark hadn't shown back up either and she couldn't help but wonder if Brooke was with him.

"Hey, Reggie," Leroy said as he walked toward her on the opposite side of the hallway. "You're not supposed to be out here."

"We're also supposed to start back up at one o'clock and it's almost two. What's going on?"

He looked at the floor. "You know I can't talk to you about stuff that goes on in chambers."

"Leroy, if it isn't about the facts of the case, I don't understand why you can't tell me. Brooke Dawson hasn't shown up yet. Can you at least tell me if she's okay?"

He stared at her for a moment, and then his shoulders sagged to signal he couldn't resist her plea. "I don't know. No one can reach her. Could be she checked out due to all the stuff that's been happening, but we've got another one missing too. Judge Hunt is trying to reach the alternate, but he's gone AWOL too. Bad coincidence."

Unless it wasn't. Reggie's mind whirred with the possibilities. She'd had a weird feeling about Mark from the moment they'd met, but she'd written it off to the clash between his busybody nature and her desire for privacy. But what if her instincts were signaling more than that? Could Benton have influenced someone else on the jury to shore up his plan?

While she digested the distasteful idea, she composed a text to Brooke. *Just checking to make sure you're okay. Not like you to be this late.* She added a zany face emoji to soften any accusatory tone in the last phrase and hit send before she could overthink the message. She stared at the screen, hoping for a quick response, but nothing appeared. While she continued to stare, the door opened, and Mark walked into the room. He nodded to Leroy and murmured that he'd run home for lunch and when he started to head back, his car wouldn't start, and he'd had to call for a ride. Reggie watched the exchange, noting the relief on Leroy's face that at least one of the wayward jurors had shown up, but the churning in her gut only accelerated. She fired off a quick text to Lennox.

Brooke is missing. Who is Mark Landon—juror? Need to know ASAP.

She didn't wait for a response and instead started googling on her own. It didn't take long to find a Mark Landon who lived in Oak Cliff and worked for a local IT company. According to his LinkedIn page, he had worked there for about five years. The house he lived in previously belonged to a woman who shared his last name—probably his mother based on the date of purchase and her best guess about Mark's age. She ran another search and confirmed Dorothy Landon, resident of Oak Cliff, had died last year and was survived by her sons, including Mark.

She stared at the screen and realized she'd found out a bunch of facts, but not a single one implied Mark would have anything to do with Brooke being a no-show. She was being overly dramatic. Anything could've made Brooke late and the simplest explanation was probably spot-on. She started to shove her phone into her pocket when it buzzed with a new text. She scanned the screen hoping it was Brooke, but it was Lennox instead.

Come see me. Now.

She looked across the room at Leroy who was still frowning, likely because Brooke hadn't turned up yet. Ducking out now would only sour his mood further, but she had no choice. She lied and told him she was going to the bathroom, but when the door shut behind her, she jogged down the back hallway and out the door on the far side that spilled into the seventh-floor hallway. Lennox's office was on the twelfth floor and she risked the elevator rather than the stairs since her heart was already racing. When she finally reached the reception desk for the DA's office, Lennox was waiting for her, car keys in hand.

"Where are you going? You told me to come see you," Reggie said, knowing she sounded annoyed, but not caring.

"Change in plans," Lennox said, already on the move. "Come on."

Reggie followed her to the back elevator that no one except the DA and judges and anyone accompanying them used. The doors opened right after Lennox pushed the button, and Reggie barely waited until the doors closed before launching in. "Tell me what's going on or I'm going to come unhinged."

Lennox stared hard at her for a moment. "You like this woman."

Reggie wanted to scream. "Are you really going to tease me right now?"

"No, but I want to warn you that I think Mark Landon is Benton's inside source and people saw Brooke leave with him at the lunch break."

Reggie's racing heart slammed still at Lennox's words. She replayed them a few times in her head, trying to make sense of the revelation. "Wait, what? Who saw Brooke leave with him? And he just came back, late, with some excuse about how he went home for lunch and then his car wouldn't start."

The elevator stopped and Lennox stepped out. "It must've started just fine because it's in the parking garage right now. Are you coming?"

Reggie followed Lennox out of the elevator, but she wasn't done asking questions. "Again, how do you know this?"

"Because Sarah has undercover agents watching all of the jurors right now."

"Including me?"

"Of course, including you. Mostly for protection, but also in case anyone started acting weird. There aren't enough agents for continuous surveillance, but they're keeping tabs on things. I figured Benton isn't the type of guy to put all his trust in one intimidated juror."

Reggie blew past dwelling on the fact she'd likely been followed and focused on Lennox's last sentence. "I don't get it. Was Mark being threatened too?" She turned the idea over in her mind, but couldn't make it work. "Wait, you think he's working for Benton."

"Bingo. His brother is a programmer who works for one of Benton's companies. Mark works freelance in IT, but Sarah did a little digging and guess where most of his contracts come from?"

"Benton Enterprises."

"You're brilliant." Lennox stopped at her car and motioned for Reggie to get in.

Reggie started to ask why nobody had caught that Mark did work for Benton during jury selection, but she knew better. The attorneys for each side only had a few minutes to review the cursory questionnaire completed by each juror and she was willing to bet Mark listed his profession, but there would've been no reason to ask about his clientele unless his work had direct bearing on the case. Add in the fact he wasn't on Benton's jury and there'd been no reason to connect Benton with the charges against Mitchell and it was easy to see how the oversight had happened.

"Are you going to tell me where we're going?"

Lennox took the bridge toward Oak Cliff. "Guess."

She didn't have to guess. "Benton's house. Do you think Brooke is there? Do you really think he would be that stupid?" she asked, while praying it was true because if Brooke wasn't there, then where was she?

"I don't know, but I need you to promise me you won't be. I shouldn't be bringing you with me, so do me a favor and hang back and let Sarah and her team do their job. She'll take care of your girl. I promise."

Reggie started to protest Lennox's characterization of Brooke, but every response she replayed in her head fell flat. Brooke might not be hers, but she couldn't deny that she wanted her to be. What would Brooke think about her showing up at Landon's, riding shotgun with the cavalry sent to save the day? Would it change her mind about whether they could have something more or would she be annoyed that Reggie kept showing up when she'd asked her for some space?

Reggie shook her head. All that mattered right now was making sure Brooke was safe. Once she was certain she was out of danger, she'd walk away, if that's what Brooke wanted, but if she was willing to try for more, she'd be ready for that too.

"Here we go," Lennox said as she pulled up to a small yellow house. "I'll go see what I can find out. Promise you'll stay in the car."

"Sure," Reggie said, secretly crossing her fingers, not wanting to fully commit. If there were clear signs Brooke was in danger, a promise to Lennox wasn't going to stop her from going in that house, FBI be damned.

At that moment, Sarah appeared and knocked on the driver's side window. Lennox lowered the window and asked, "What's up?"

"No one's here," Sarah said, her face grim.

"What do you mean?" Reggie asked. "Then where is she?"

"I mean no one's here." Sarah sighed. "Brooke was with him when he stopped by here, but Landon lost my guy on his way back to the courthouse. We assumed he'd left her here since she wasn't with him when he showed up in the parking garage, but I guess it's possible he took her somewhere else on the way."

Reggie came out of her seat. "You assume? You guess?" She turned to Lennox. "What the hell? She could be anywhere. He could have…"

She couldn't allow herself to speak the words for fear saying them might create a reality she couldn't face. A moment ago, she'd been ready to charge the house if there were signs Brooke was in trouble, but now she knew she was and she had no idea where to go or what to do to make it right. All she knew for sure was finding Brooke was the most important thing she could do and if these people couldn't do it, she would take matters into her own hands.

CHAPTER EIGHTEEN

Brooke woke up to the sound of footfalls and a sharp pain bit into her joints jolting her memory. She was gagged and blindfolded with her legs tied to a chair and her hands were bound behind her back. She cried out, but the muffled sounds were barely audible to her own ears—whoever was outside the door had no chance of hearing her pleas. Before she could come up with an alternate plan, she heard the footsteps fade into the distance along with any hope she might be rescued.

After a few moments of pointless struggle, she leaned into the silence, listening for a clue, any clue about what was happening to her. At first she was discouraged with only the sound of the air conditioner whirring to life—not much of a clue, but then she was grateful that wherever she was being held, at least she had some small creature comfort.

An image of Mark's face flashed in her mind, and she wondered how she'd completely missed that he was dangerous from the start. *You're a bad judge of character*, said the voice inside her head that constantly barraged her about the messiness of her life. But the other voice, the one that told her to be kind to herself, replied, *How could you know he was bad? Besides, you like Reggie and she's a stellar human.*

But you pushed Reggie away.

Win one for the accusatory inner voice. Time to shut down this game because she wasn't going to find a way out of here by second-guessing her decisions. And she had to get out of here. Ben would probably be out of school soon. Who would look out for him if something happened to her? Who would protect him if he was in danger?

She shook away the dread and wished she could rip away the blindfold. The dark canvas was an invitation to think the worst and her thoughts were bleak enough already. Despair began to creep in. Her sense of time was skewed by the drug, but it felt like hours since she'd left the courthouse with Mark, and hope was fading fast.

Her brain raced through a succession of nightmare scenarios, all of which left Ben without a parent. She should've planned better, made sure she had people in her life who would be willing and able to step up if anything ever happened to her, but she'd been too focused on what she needed to do—get her degree, get a real job that paid real money—and somewhere along the way, she'd forgotten there was an actual reason she was working so hard, sacrificing so much. Hell, she'd even pushed away the one person who'd seen her life up close and hadn't run far and fast in the opposite direction.

Where was Reggie right now? Was she back at the courthouse having a side convo with Leroy about the silly juror who'd gone to lunch and hadn't come back? Had the judge let the proceedings start back up without her or had everything come to a screeching halt in her absence?

You're not that important. The voice inside her conjured the statement from a sinister mix of exes and fake parents who'd told her the same. Surely that was why she'd been picked in the first place. She'd been targeted for being the calm one, the one who smoothed things over, who went along to get along. The one who didn't have anyone else in her life to turn to when her child was threatened and could be counted on to comply with any instructions if it meant keeping Ben safe.

What would Reggie do if she knew what was happening right now? Flashes of Reggie driving full speed to the hospital and barreling past all obstacles to get to Ben told her exactly what she needed to know. Reggie would be there for her, in good times and bad, strong and fierce. She'd pushed her away because she was used to doing everything on her own, even figured she had to in order to prove her own worth, but maybe there was a greater value in letting her guard down and accepting love from someone else. And now she might not get the chance.

She sat in silence for a moment, replaying the last few times she'd seen Reggie, wishing she'd let the future simply play out instead of orchestrating it to the only conclusion she thought she deserved.

A low whistle broke into her thoughts, and she stiffened at the sound. She didn't know the tune, but she recognized the whistler and braced for Mark to enter the room. Whatever he had planned, she was ready for him, and she would not go down without a fight.

❖

Reggie's hand was on the car door handle ready for the second Lennox stopped the car in front of Ben's school. As the vehicle eased to the curb, she lost her patience and opened the door only to feel Lennox grab her other arm.

"Slow your roll. School's in session and the resource officer confirmed he's in class."

Reggie shook off Lennox's arm. "Sure, but every minute Brooke is missing means this kid could wind up without a parent. I hope you brought your badge." She didn't wait for a response before jumping out of the car and jogging to the front door of the school. She'd made it a few steps inside when she heard footsteps behind her and turned to see Lennox running toward her. She held the door as Lennox dashed past.

"Come on," Lennox called out. "Let's do this."

Relieved not to have to tackle this job on her own, Reggie followed Lennox to the administrative office. Sarah and her team were still in Oak Cliff, regrouping in their efforts to find Brooke, but Reggie had insisted on seeing Ben herself, to be sure he wasn't in any danger and so the questions came from a familiar face. Besides, if there was a chance Brooke wasn't in trouble, but had simply decided not to come back to court, Ben might have some idea of where she might be.

Lennox handled the introductions at the front desk and the secretary motioned for them to have a seat. Reggie was too jacked up to sit and started pacing the room, acutely aware she was making the staff uncomfortable, but not caring enough to stop. She was on her third pass when she heard someone call her name and she looked up to see Ben walking toward her.

"Hi, Reggie!" His face broke out into a big smile. "Did you come to watch the mathlete practice?"

She returned his smile to cover the gut punch of guilt. Here he was thinking her visit was a fun surprise when it was anything but. "Hey, Ben, I wish." She pointed at the chair next to Lennox and when he was seated, she took the one on the other side. "Court let out early today and I need to reach your mom, but her phone battery died while she was telling me where she was. Any chance you could give me a rundown of any places she might be?"

He put a finger on his chin while he pondered her question, and she resisted the urge to shake him to get a faster response.

"I guess she could be at the restaurant," he said. "Or she could be at the library. She likes to go to the library at Richards to study. She says it's because they don't let you use phones in there so she doesn't get the urge to play Candy Crush instead of focusing on her homework."

He grinned to punctuate the remark and Reggie wanted to scoop him up and tell him everything would be okay, but he wasn't the one who needed the reassurance—she did. She shot a look at Lennox who nodded her support. "Thanks, Ben. Any place else you can think of?"

He shook his head. "I'll let you know if I think of anything." He pointed at her phone. She handed it over and watched while he entered his phone number. "And you can text me anytime you want. But not during class. Or mathlete practice. Or meets. Okay?"

She reached out and ruffled his hair. "Okay. You better get back to class."

"Yep." He stood and gave her a mock salute. "Thanks for coming to see me."

She waited until he was halfway down the hall before turning to Lennox. "Sarah's got someone here watching him, right?"

Lennox jerked her chin at a woman who was following Ben. "On it."

Reggie had seen the woman when they'd walked in and figured she was a teacher or staff, but now she noticed the authoritative way she strode down the hall, her gaze sweeping back and forth. "Good." She checked the time. "What are we going to do when school's out and we still don't know where Brooke is?"

"You're forgetting mathlete practice. That'll keep him busy for a bit. In the meantime…" A loud ringtone interrupted her words, drawing attention from the woman at the front desk who frowned and held a finger to her mouth. Lennox pointed at the door and Reggie followed her outside where she impatiently listened to one side of the conversation.

"Not there either?…Did you check the library?…What about—okay, fine. We'll see what else we can find out." Lennox disconnected the call and shook her head.

"They can't find her," Reggie said, hating the declaration but needing to hear Lennox confirm her worst fear.

"They can't. She's not at work, not at the library, not at home."

"Has anyone questioned Benton?"

"Not a good idea. First, he's in the middle of a trial, but even so, if he suspects we're on to him, he might do something stupid."

Reggie clenched her fists. "Put me in a room with him for five minutes and I'll have an answer."

"And a mistrial in his case too." Lennox motioned for Reggie to get in the car. "Cool your jets and let's think this through. If Mark didn't leave her at his house, where could he have taken her?"

"Good question." Reggie's mind whirred with possibilities, but her thoughts kept coming back to one key fact. "Mark was late getting back from lunch, but only by a few minutes."

"Your point?"

Reggie pulled out her phone and put in Mark's address. She clicked on the map that appeared as the first entry and zoomed in on his house. "If he stopped on the way back, it was a quick in and out. They searched the entire house?"

"Yes. They didn't find anything suspect."

Reggie stared at the image on her phone for a moment and then pinched the corners and drew them back in to zoom out and then she zoomed back in again. She repeated the process a couple of times.

"Care to share?" Lennox asked.

Reggie pointed at the yellow bungalow and drew her finger across the map. "Look at this. Mark's yard backs right up to this building." She enlarged the map again. "I know this building. It used to be loft apartments and it was converted into an office building last year." Her thoughts started to snowball and her fingers couldn't keep up as she typed another search into her phone. A few more clicks and she found exactly what she was looking for. "There! That's it." She shoved the phone at Lennox. It took her a moment, but when she finally got it her eyes lit up.

"Holy shit."

"I know, right?"

"We've got to get back to the courthouse. I'll call Judge Hunt on the way."

CHAPTER NINETEEN

"My client was here at the courthouse all morning," Gloria Leland practically shouted the words while waving her arms to emphasize the point. "But you think she somehow spirited away a juror and hid her at one of her office buildings?"

Reggie wanted to shout back, but since she shouldn't even be in the room, she kept her cool and let Lennox do the talking.

"Brooke Dawson was last seen mere feet from your client's office building. She's received threats designed to influence deliberations. She's disappeared, and her disappearance could result in a mistrial which benefits one person—your client." Lennox ticked each of the points off on her fingers. "It's easy for your client to prove there's nothing nefarious going on. All she has to do is let us search her building."

"In front of clients and employees," Leland sneered. "Right. You can't put Ms. Mitchell away so you try to ruin her business instead."

"She's doing that on her own without any help from us by joining forces with Harry Benton."

"Okay, that's enough," Judge Hunt said, smacking his palm on his desk like a makeshift gavel. He turned to Lennox. "If you have enough to get a warrant, bring it to me."

"We do and I will," Lennox said. "Just figured I'd give her the benefit of the doubt and let her cooperate on her own." She stood and motioned to Reggie to follow.

"Wait."

Reggie's back was to Mitchell, but she heard the defeat infused in the one word.

"You can search, but do it quietly please," Mitchell said. "Half the building is empty, but I can't afford to lose more tenants at the rates this one is charging me." Mitchell pointed at Leland who merely shrugged.

Lennox put a fist in the air. "Perfect. We'll start there."

She dashed out of the room and Reggie was right behind her. "What's the plan?" she asked as they boarded the elevator to the parking garage.

"We'll call Sarah from the car, but she's already got a team lined up to help us execute the warrant we no longer need. It'll be better this way because we can go in unannounced."

Reggie nodded and started thinking of ways she could get in Mitchell's building without being noticed.

"I know what you're thinking," Lennox said. "Sarah will never let you in there."

The declaration was a challenge. "You can get me in."

"No can do. It's bad enough I'm involving you at all."

"Seriously?" Reggie's anger sparked and she could barely contain the rage she'd been holding back. "You really think it's going to matter that you let a juror get involved in this investigation when it's pretty damn clear Mitchell's trial can't go forward under any circumstances? One of the jurors is freaking missing and if she doesn't show up soon, a mistrial isn't going to be the worst thing that will happen." Her voice cracked, but she forced the next words. "I didn't get a chance to tell her how I feel. I…"

She stopped short because she couldn't say the words out loud. Not to Lennox first anyway. She balled her fists and stared hard, daring Lennox to fight her on this, but Lennox stepped into her space and clapped her on the shoulder.

"I'd be saying the exact same thing if Wren were in trouble." The doors to the elevator opened and she motioned for Reggie to go first. "Come on, you can come with, but you're going to have to trust the rest of us to find your girl."

Reggie led the way, determined that by the time they got to Mitchell's building, she would find a way to be part of the charge. Brooke wasn't her girl yet, but the minute they made sure she was safe and sound, she was going to do everything in her power to make that happen.

❖

The clink of a key jammed into the lock, a hard click as it turned, and then the loud whoosh of a door swinging wide. With the blindfold on, Brooke could spend a moment imagining that whoever was coming through that door was someone else— someone come to rescue her—but when Mark spoke, she was certain her fate was sealed.

"You're awake. Must've been a bad batch."

Footsteps slapped toward her and suddenly the blindfold was ripped away. She squinted at the light until she could fully focus on his cold, dead eyes. Gone was the socially awkward, but friendly veneer, replaced with callous disregard. He didn't see her as a person, only a means to an end, but she still couldn't figure out his angle.

"I'll take out the gag if you promise not to yell." He waited until she nodded and then loosened the piece of cloth, letting it fall around her neck.

"Can I have something to drink?" Brooke asked, as much of a test of his humanity as to quench her thirst.

He walked over to a desk across the room and retrieved a bottle of water. She used the moment his back was turned to survey her surroundings. It appeared they were in an office, but if it belonged to someone, that person didn't waste time on making the space personal inadvertently thwarting her attempt to find a clue to where she was being held.

When he turned back toward her, she quickly jerked her gaze away from the desk and focused on the water. She was parched and eagerly swallowed several gulps from the upended bottle of water until he pulled it away.

"That's enough. Next, you'll want to use the bathroom and that's not in my job description."

She seized on the words. "So, this is a job for you? Are you being paid to kidnap me?"

He laughed. "You weren't kidnapped. You went to lunch with me willingly. I'm certain there are many people who would testify to that fact. We had an amicable lunch, but after I dropped you back at the courthouse, you vanished, flaking out on your jury duty." He smirked. "I mean you were late almost every day, it's not like people aren't going to believe you didn't want to be there in the first place."

Could he seriously not realize the judge already knew she'd been threatened? If he was working for Mitchell or Harry Benton, they obviously hadn't been keeping him in the loop. She debated whether or not to say anything. If she let him know people might be looking for her, would he be more inclined to let her go?

Probably not. He might not be fully in the loop, but after what he'd done so far, he had to know she'd go straight to the police and his "job" would likely end with a prison sentence. The best thing she could do right now was to keep him talking until she could figure out a way to escape.

"What's next?" When he didn't immediately respond, she said, "Are you planning on leaving me here or are you taking me somewhere else?"

He wagged a finger in front of her face. "Don't worry. This will all be over for you soon. If you'd done what you were told to do in the first place, then you wouldn't be in this position."

His words signaled he knew something about how she'd been threatened and that she'd chosen not to cave, leading her to believe he may not be simply a lackey hired to spirit her away. If that was the case, he had even more motivation not to let her go. She could think of only one way out and it was a long shot, but the only one she had.

"You're right," she said, bowing her head both to hide any expression that might belie her words and convince him she was contrite. "I made a mistake. A big one." She paused for a moment and then lifted her head and looked him straight in the eye. "Give me another chance and I'll make it right. Whatever you need me to do."

He threw his head back and laughed. The sound was eerie and unnatural and as much as she wanted it to stop, she feared what would come next, but in the meantime, she used the cover of his crazy to work at the bonds on her hands knowing this might very well be her last chance to escape. She'd just started to feel some slack when his laughter abruptly stopped.

"Did you hear that?" he asked, cocking his head toward the door.

How could I when you're making so much noise, she wanted to say, but she merely followed his gaze. She didn't hear anything. "I think so," she lied. "But I'm not surprised. I heard people walking around several times while you were gone."

He narrowed his eyes. "Doubtful. This entire floor is empty. No one would be up here."

"Where is here?" She kept her tone nonchalant, like they were acquaintances having a conversation about the weather, hoping she could lull him into answering.

"Wouldn't you like to know?"

So much for that. She shrugged and took a different tack. "Can you blame me? I figure you're not letting me out of here alive, right? Maybe I just want to know more about where I'm going to die."

He grunted, but she could tell she'd gotten to him. This guy might be off balance, but he wasn't a murderer and she suspected he might be in deeper than he'd planned so she pushed on. "I mean you don't have much choice, right? I've seen your face and I'm sure it's some kind of federal offense to tamper with a jury, let alone kidnap a juror and hold her against her will."

"Like I said before, I didn't kidnap you. You came with me *willingly.*"

His extra emphasis on the last word didn't change the fact he didn't seem as confident now as he had when he'd spewed the same nonsense earlier. "I don't think the federal agents are going to see it the same way," she pushed.

"So, I should kill you right now?" he jeered.

Tricky question and she had to navigate the rest of this conversation carefully. "Maybe not right now. I mean, have you accomplished what you set out to do?" She cocked her head. "And what is that exactly? Are you working for Mitchell or Benton? Or both?"

For a second it looked like he wanted to engage, but instead he started pacing. She watched him walk back and forth several times and wondered if each pass was a countdown to her demise. She contemplated asking him something else to distract him from whatever plot might be forming in his head, but before she could form the words, he suddenly stopped.

"Yes!" he said in a eureka moment.

"Yes?"

"Yes, I've accomplished what I set out to do." He took a step toward her. "And now it's time to eliminate the loose ends."

He pulled a pistol from his pocket and pointed it toward her as he came closer. She'd grossly underestimated his commitment to whatever this was and she needed a quick pivot if she was going to survive. She strained against her bonds, not giving a shit about the warm trickle of blood running into her palms. "Wait," she begged him. "There's a way out of this that doesn't involve killing me."

"I'm sure you wish there was."

"If you fire that gun, someone's going to hear it."

"I'll be long gone before they find you."

She scrambled for something else to say, but he was coming closer, pistol still trained on her and she knew no words were going to stop him. She rocked forward, ready to body slam him, chair and all, but before she could make her move, the door burst open full force and loud shouts filled the air.

CHAPTER TWENTY

R eggie had her hand on the door handle of the car, ready to jump out the second Lennox stopped the car.

"Don't even think about it," Lennox said.

"Oh, I'm going to do more than think about it. Besides, you brought me along. Did you seriously think I was going to wait in the car? Would you?"

"I said I understood why you wanted to go in, but this is Sarah's operation. I'll do everything in my power to get you inside, but it's her call."

Reggie nodded, but she was already formulating a plan on her own. She promised Lennox she'd wait in the car while she went and talked to Sarah, but the minute Lennox was out of sight, she ducked out the door and dashed around the side of the building, looking for a back door.

She found one within seconds, but not on her own, as she watched a guy in a hoodie glance around and then duck behind the brick wall surrounding the dumpsters and disappear from sight. She ran over to see where he'd gone and showed up just in time to see a door slowly swinging toward the building, about an inch from closing shut. She jammed her hand into the doorway and pulled hard, propping the door open with one of the bricks lying nearby, just in case she needed to make a quick escape.

The hallway was dark and industrial looking. She used her phone for a flashlight and shined the light a few feet ahead. No doors and no sign of the guy she'd followed in. She had two choices. Go back outside, find Lennox and Sarah and tell them about the guy, or plunge ahead and assess the situation for herself.

If you were a PI working on a hot case, would you sit around and wait for the cops or check it out yourself?

She spent a split-second wondering what Skye Keaton would do and she knew she'd do exactly the same thing. She cupped her hand over her phone to dim the light and quickly but quietly stepped through the corridor, edging past a pile of boxes and praying she didn't make any noise.

She needn't have worried since a quick glance around told her she was alone. Whoever the guy was that she'd followed in had disappeared fast, like he was on a mission and Reggie knew in her gut the mission was Brooke.

When she reached the end of the hallway, she found a door to a stairwell and an elevator. The directory next to the elevator told her she was on the first floor and the only other thing located there was the lobby. She started to press the up button for the elevator, but quickly decided the stairway was a better option and less likely to announce her arrival. She started climbing, stopping at the landing between floors to make sure no one else was in the space. When she reached the second floor, she pressed her ear against the door before pushing it open, praying no one was waiting on the other side, but when she crossed the threshold someone grabbed her by the shoulder and pushed her back into the stairwell. She started to push back before she realized the someone was Lennox.

"What the hell are you doing?" Lennox hissed.

"Same as you, apparently." She pointed at the door. "Having a look around. Were you going to come back and get me or leave me wondering what's going on?"

"I told you, everything about this search is Sarah's call and she nixed you being in the building for obvious reasons." Lennox shook her head. "And I knew you'd come anyway."

"Just like you would if Wren went missing." Reggie was prepared to do battle over her right to be here. "It's a building open to the public and I'm a member of the public. Are you going to argue with me or help me find Brooke?"

Lennox paused only a moment before pointing at the door. "I've already checked out the rooms on the left side of the hall. Let's tag team the ones on the right."

Reggie clapped her on the shoulder, grateful for the friendship and even more grateful not to have to search for Brooke on her own, partly because she could use the help, but mostly because she was worried about what she might find. Anger swelled within her. Anger at the threats on Brooke's and her son's lives. Anger about the shooting last year. She was ready to unleash some of her pent-up rage, and if Brooke was hurt, she would find that fucker Mark and take him and anyone else who was involved down.

The corridor was quiet, and she signaled to Lennox that she'd check out the doors on the right side. The first office was completely empty—no desks, no chairs, and nothing in the storage closet. The second and third ones were sparsely furnished, but the lack of any buzzing machines or strewn about office supplies seemed to signal no one was using them. Was the rest of the building like this? Where were all the tenants Mitchell had been worried would be disturbed by the police presence? How good a businessperson was Mitchell or Benton if this prime piece of real estate was practically empty?

Back in the hall, she looked around for Lennox, wanting to ask her if the offices downstairs were as empty as the ones up here, but Lennox was nowhere in sight. She started to cross the hallway to look for her when she heard a weird sound, like an overly exaggerated laugh on a haunted house soundtrack. She stayed perfectly still for a moment, trying to figure out which direction the sound was coming from, but the sound had faded to silence, and she was left guessing where to turn. She closed her eyes for a moment and focused on the memory of what she'd heard, finally deciding the sound had come from a bit farther down the hall. She stood outside the office door two down from where she'd last searched, careful to keep silent. Her care was rewarded a moment later when she heard Mark's unmistakable voice asking someone if they'd heard anything and she instantly knew that someone was Brooke.

As if summoned, Lennox appeared in the hallway and Reggie quickly put a finger over her lips when she noticed Lennox about to say something. She pointed at the door with her free hand and mouthed. *She's in there with Mark*, hoping Lennox understood.

Lennox nodded. She pulled her phone from her pocket and pointed at the screen, typing with determination before shoving it her way. *I'll go get Sarah. You wait here. Don't go in until I get back.*

Reggie watched her go, content to lose her company if it meant she wasn't being watched, and determined not to wait a second longer if it meant leaving Brooke in danger. She pressed her ear against the door, but the conversation had gotten muffled, and she could only pick up a word here and there—*federal offense, kidnap, willingly*. Mostly Brooke's voice. She sounded cool and calm, but Reggie detected an undercurrent of worry. When she heard Mark say, "So, I should kill you now," she stiffened with panic. Where the hell were Lennox and Sarah?

She stared at her phone. There was no message and no time for a back-and-forth exchange. She knew what she needed to do and the fact she didn't have a weapon or the backing of a posse of federal agents wasn't going to stop her. Slowly and carefully, she reached for the doorknob and twisted it, relieved to find it wasn't locked. She had two choices, slip in and hope she could enter the room undetected or burst through the door and make enough noise to create a giant distraction and convince Mark she was accompanied by a team of agents.

There really wasn't a choice at all. She took a few steps back to give herself space for a running start and then shot forward. When her shoulder connected with the door, she yelled with as much ferocity as she could muster. "Police! Drop your weapon or we'll shoot!"

❖

Brooke strained to see around Mark, allowing herself to be hopeful for the first time that afternoon, but instead of a cavalry of federal agents showing up to save the day, Reggie stood alone in the doorway looking ferocious and wonderful, but also completely vulnerable considering Mark's gun was now trained on her.

Reggie raised her hands in the air. "You're going to want to drop that gun," she said.

"I don't think so." Mark laughed. "I knew you had a crush on her, but this is seriously over the top." He motioned for her to hand him her phone, and then turned and pointed to a spot next to Brooke. "Go over there and stay put. You like her so much, you may as well spend your last moments with her."

Brooke kept her eyes on Reggie as she walked over, willing her to see the gratitude she felt for Reggie's attempt to save her and the regret for putting her in this situation. She never should've let Reggie get close, never should've involved her in her problems. She'd spent her life working things out on her own and now it was going to end with the one person by her side who'd made her feel like she deserved to have a partner who could share in life's ups and downs before she'd ever really had a chance to fully appreciate their time together.

She mouthed "I'm sorry," but Reggie mouthed back "Don't be" and then smiled to punctuate the words. How could Reggie be so calm right now? Was she always this unflappable or was she pretending to make her feel better? Either way, Brooke mourned the chance she'd blown to be with Reggie, to take their relationship to the next level. Reggie was a keeper, but she'd kept her at a distance. Big. Mistake.

"Last chance," Reggie said, directing her words at Mark. "Let us walk out of here and you might have enough leverage to keep from going to prison for the rest of your life."

Mark laughed again. "I'm not going to prison. Prison is for people who don't have important friends."

"Nope. Prison is for people just like you and Harry Benton. He's going down and so will you."

"You're just saying that because you think he's responsible for you getting shot."

"I know he's responsible for me getting shot and other people dying."

Mark shook the gun. "Then you know I'm serious when I tell you you're not leaving here."

Reggie raised her hands again and pointed at Brooke. "I'll stay, but let her go. You don't need us both and she's got a kid."

Brooke bit back a cry of protest. She didn't want Reggie to sacrifice herself, but she was all Ben had. If something happened to her, she didn't even want to consider what might become of him. Still, she couldn't let Reggie take that on. Hell, Reggie wouldn't be in this position if not for her, so it was up to her to make sure she didn't suffer more because of it, but before she could say anything Mark sealed both their fates.

"You must think I'm an idiot," he said. "Like either one of you wouldn't go straight to the cops if I let you walk out of here."

He motioned for Reggie to stand next to Brooke. "Give me a minute and I'll figure out what to do with you both."

Brooke watched Reggie walk toward her, desperate to say something, but when she opened her mouth, Reggie frowned and cut her eyes toward Mark. She was right. The words she wanted to say weren't ones she cared for Mark to witness. She'd save them for later and pray there would be time for more.

When Reggie reached her side, she reached back and gave her hand a quick squeeze and all she could think about was that there was no one she'd rather be in this situation with. She looked across the room at Mark who was busy texting someone on his phone and took a risk. "I hate that you're here, but I couldn't be more grateful."

"Nowhere I'd rather be," Reggie whispered back.

Considering their situation, it was a total lie, but also the perfect thing to say which only matched pretty much everything else about her. "I'm afraid we're not getting out of here alive."

"We are. Lennox and Sarah are in the building. They'll find us soon." Reggie dropped her voice a bit lower. "Besides, I promised Ben nothing would happen to you."

Brooke scrambled for a breath. "He's okay?"

"Safe and sound."

The tension she'd been holding all day dropped a notch and it was replaced with a renewed confidence. "We have to get out of here so you can keep that promise. He's big on people keeping their promises."

Reggie nodded. "And I'm big on keeping mine. Trust me?"

"Hundred percent." The commitment should've surprised her, but it didn't. She didn't know when her fear had shifted into full scale head over heels, but she knew one thing for sure. She would follow Reggie through fire.

"Stop talking." Mark hissed the words at them, but he was still staring at his phone.

CARSEN TAITE

"What's the matter?" Reggie asked. "Your buddies aren't rushing to help you out of the mess they got you into? Are you always the guy who gets stuck standing alone when the trouble stops being fun? The cops are on their way and they're not any locals your buddy Benton might be able to con into letting you off the hook. It's the feds and you're going away for a pretty lengthy stretch. No parole from federal prison. Flip on your pals and you might get a break."

He slammed his phone down on the nearest desk. "Shut up, shut up, shut up."

Brooke flinched at the anger in his tone, but she'd pledged her trust to Reggie, and she was committed to following her lead. As if she could hear her thoughts, Reggie shot her a look of "I got this," and stepped closer into Mark's space.

"Leave now and you might have a chance." She looked at her watch. "They should be about done searching the other floors by now."

"You're bluffing. If you had cops in the building, you would've waited for them before charging in here or at least texted them before you decided to go rogue."

"Maybe I did." Reggie grinned and pointed at the phone lying on the table next to his. "Why don't you see for yourself."

Mark tripped over his confident swagger as he rushed to pick up the phone. He held it up to Reggie's face to unlock the screen and started jabbing his forefinger on it in a desperate search for information even though it might be too late to be of any use. Brooke's eyes were on him, so she didn't notice when Reggie went into motion, but she saw the blur of her body lunging toward Mark, knocking the phone out of his hand as they tumbled to the floor. She rose from her chair, forgetting she was still strapped securely to it, and stumbled forward, a heavy, awkward useless effort to come to Reggie's aid. She'd barely made it two steps before she heard a loud bang and the room went still.

She stared at the floor, at Mark and Reggie lying in a tangled heap with a trail of blood snaking out from the space between them. She heard shouts in the distance along with repeated hard slaps of footfalls running toward her, but it was all a distant echo against the backdrop of a piercing scream.

It wasn't until the door burst open again that she realized the scream was her own and the second she did, she crumpled to the floor.

CHAPTER TWENTY-ONE

Reggie grabbed the icepack from the nurse and swung her legs off the bed. "I'm good now."

The nurse placed a hand on her chest and pushed her backward with surprising force. "You're not, actually. And you're not leaving this room until the doctor releases you."

She formulated a half dozen responses, but none seemed likely to change this woman's mind. Fine, she'd wait until her captor was gone and make a break for it. Brooke was out there somewhere, and she had to get to her.

"Don't even think about it," the nurse said. "We'll all be keeping an eye on you. We've got strict orders to keep you safe."

Reggie's brain was too foggy to fully process the words, but she decided to let it go and bide her time. They couldn't keep her here forever, right?

"Fighting with the nurses?" a voice from the hallway called out. "Not the best way to get the good-flavored pudding."

Reggie looked around the nurse to see Lennox leaning against the doorway. "Get in here and tell this woman I can leave."

"She's not going to do that," the nurse replied.

"Why not?"

"Because she's the one who ordered me to keep you here."
She pointed at Lennox. "She flashed her badge and said you were
a very important witness in a high-profile case and you just saved
someone's life."

"Is that right?" Reggie directed the question at Lennox.
"Because if all of that is true, she should know there's somewhere
I have to be right now and it's very important."

Lennox stepped aside to reveal Brooke standing behind her.
"I think you mean there's someone you have to see right now.
And the reason I needed you to stay put is so I could bring her to
you without you getting in the middle of any gunfire."

Reggie heard the words, but they barely registered as she
locked eyes with Brooke and made a silent vow to never let go.
"Lennox, I need you to take this lovely nurse and leave us alone
for a minute."

Lennox grinned. "On it." She motioned for Brooke to enter
the room. "She's all yours. She's a handful, but I have a feeling
you got this."

"Trust me, I know what I'm getting into, and I wouldn't
have it any other way."

As Brooke started toward her, Reggie stood, intending to
meet her halfway, but the pain in the back of her head swirled up
into a searing storm and she lost her balance. Instantly, Brooke
was at her side, holding her arm, and easing her back onto the
bed. She politely, but firmly ordered the nurse to find another ice
pack and curled up against her on the bed. Brooke's embrace was
strong and warm, and she never wanted it to end. After a minute
of silence, Brooke sighed prompting her to ask, "Are you okay?"

"I'm fine. You're the one who was launching yourself into
gunfire." Brooke kissed her lightly on the cheek. "I'm so relieved
you're alright."

Alright didn't accurately describe how she felt right now.
The adrenaline from the ordeal had dissipated and now that she

was safely wrapped in Brooke's arms, the rest of her energy receded. "Same to you," she said, barely suppressing a yawn.

Brooke narrowed her eyes. "You're tired. Of course you are." She edged away. "I should go and let you rest."

Reggie reached for her hand. "Please stay." She watched Brooke's face, noting the slight frown. She probably had other places to be, like at home with her son. "Sorry, that was selfish. You should be with Ben."

"Ben is fine. As much as I want to keep him close, we need to be able to decompress about what happened and I don't want him to ever know how close he got to losing me. Your pal Lennox and her girlfriend are taking him for the night." Brooke smiled. "Besides, I get the impression it was a combination let's let them have some alone time and let's see if we want one of our own someday." She shrugged. "Either way, you have me all to yourself. Should we break you out of here or are you sold on hanging out for the possibility of pudding?"

"Break out, please."

"Good answer. I'm going to find the doctor and make it so."

Reggie watched her leave the room, missing her company within seconds. She reached back and touched the bandage on her head and winced at the sharp pain the gentle touch provoked. She was in no shape to do the things she wanted to do with Brooke, but she was grateful for the prospect of having time alone with her now that the threat of recent days was behind them. She wanted to know more about the trial and Benton and everything else, but right now she couldn't bring herself to care about anything but the very next step and she was going to take it with Brooke.

An hour later, after a skirmish with the nursing staff at the hospital and a few rounds with the doctor on call, they pulled up in front of her apartment building. Brooke parked in the spot closest to her apartment and came around to help her out of the car. She placed one arm gently around her waist and led her to the door. Reggie fished in her pocket for the key and handed it to Brooke, happy to let her take control.

Once inside, Reggie sank onto the couch with a sigh, her body aching but her mind still buzzing from the intensity of the day. She glanced around, relieved to see the apartment was tidy, and gave Brooke a grateful smile. "Sorry, I'm not much of a hostess on a good day. There's Coke in the fridge though. I might be addicted."

Brooke smiled back, her eyes soft as she grabbed two bottles from the fridge. "No need to play hostess. You've been through enough today." She handed one to Reggie and sat down beside her. "Mind if I join you?"

"Of course not." Reggie took a sip of the drink and sank deeper into the cushions. For a moment, they sat in comfortable silence, the tension from earlier slowly fading away, replaced by a quiet warmth.

"This is nice," Reggie murmured.

Brooke slid a little closer, their legs brushing. "This is nicer," she said softly, clinking her bottle against Reggie's. She hesitated, then reached out, taking Reggie's hand in her own. "I don't know what I would've done if you hadn't shown up."

Reggie shook her head. "You would've figured it out. You always do."

"Maybe," Brooke admitted, her thumb brushing softly over Reggie's knuckles. "But I'm tired of doing everything on my own."

"You don't have to anymore," Reggie said, her voice steady as she met Brooke's eyes. She squeezed her hand, feeling the weight of everything she wanted to say but not yet knowing how. "I'm falling in love with you, Brooke."

The words hung in the air, and for a moment, Brooke simply stared at her, as if processing. But then a soft smile spread across her lips, and she leaned in, brushing her lips against Reggie's. "I've been falling for you too," she whispered.

Reggie's heart swelled with the admission, and she kissed Brooke again, more deeply this time. The tenderness between them was palpable, but there was also something electric simmering just beneath the surface. Brooke's hands trailed down Reggie's shoulders, lingering near her injury, her touch light but full of intent.

"Are you okay?" Brooke whispered, pausing as if to make sure she wasn't causing Reggie any pain.

Reggie tugged her closer, her body humming with desire. "I'm okay. Just be gentle."

Brooke nodded, her movements careful but deliberate as she leaned in again, kissing her deeply. Their lips moved in sync, slow and exploratory at first, but with a growing intensity that neither of them could ignore. Reggie slid her hands around Brooke's waist, pulling her even closer, and Brooke responded eagerly, her body pressing against Reggie's with soft urgency.

As their kisses deepened, Brooke's hands moved with increasing confidence, exploring Reggie's body with a mixture of curiosity and reverence. She was careful around Reggie's injury, her fingers trailing lightly over her side, but she made up for it with her tenderness, her touch igniting a fire inside Reggie that had been simmering since the moment they'd met.

Reggie's breath hitched as Brooke's hand dipped beneath her shirt, her fingers tracing the skin just above her waist. "You're incredible," Reggie murmured between kisses, her voice thick with emotion.

Brooke smiled against her lips, her breath coming faster now. "You're just saying that because you want me to keep kissing you."

Reggie laughed softly, tugging Brooke closer. "Maybe. But I also think you're incredible without the kissing." She pulled back slightly, enough to meet Brooke's gaze. "You're raising a great kid, going back to school, working so hard, and you still manage to be this strong, amazing woman."

A faint frown flashed across Brooke's face, and she glanced away. Reggie reached out and cradled her cheek until Brooke faced her again. "Did I say something wrong?"

Brooke hunched her shoulders. "I've got a lot going on and I'm totally okay with that, and you're great with Ben, but have you seriously thought about what it means that I have a kid?"

Reggie laughed again. "Uh, I have seen mama bear in action. Up close and personal." She paused for emphasis. "The way you love Ben, the lengths you would go to protect him? Those things only make me fall for you more."

Brooke's eyes softened at the words, and she leaned in, her lips brushing against Reggie's once more, this time with more intensity, as if words were no longer enough to express how she felt. She kissed her harder, her hands moving to the hem of Reggie's shirt, tugging it up slowly.

Reggie allowed her to pull the shirt over her head, her breath coming in short, shallow bursts as Brooke's hands moved over her skin, caressing her carefully, but with growing confidence. Brooke's lips followed the path of her hands, trailing soft kisses along Reggie's neck, her collarbone, and down to her chest. Each touch evoking a wave of pleasure, her body responding eagerly to Brooke's tenderness.

"You're beautiful," Brooke whispered, her voice husky as she looked up at Reggie, her fingers tracing the curve of her waist.

Reggie's breath caught at the look in Brooke's eyes, and she leaned forward, pulling Brooke into another searing kiss. "So are you," she murmured against Brooke's lips, her hands moving to the buttons of Brooke's shirt, her fingers trembling slightly as she undid them one by one.

When Brooke's shirt fell away, Reggie let her hands explore, savoring the warmth of Brooke's skin beneath her palms. She was careful, mindful of her own injury, but the desire between them was undeniable, and soon they were both lost in the feel of each other.

Brooke's hands roamed lower, her touch soft but insistent as she pressed Reggie back onto the bed, never breaking the intensity of their connection. Reggie's body responded instinctively, arching into Brooke's touch, her breath coming in short gasps as pleasure built between them.

Their touch became more urgent, their bodies moving in perfect rhythm as they explored each other, their kisses growing deeper, more passionate. Reggie pulled Brooke closer, and Brooke's breath hitched as she pressed her hips against Reggie's, their bodies perfectly aligned.

"Are you okay?" Brooke asked again, her voice breathless but full of concern as she paused, her fingers trailing lightly over Reggie's side.

Reggie nodded, her body trembling with anticipation. "I'm perfect," she whispered, her hands sliding up to cup Brooke's face, pulling her into another kiss. "I want this. I want you."

Brooke leaned down, her lips capturing hers in a searing kiss. Their rhythm resumed instantly, and passionate, intense touches sent Reggie close to the edge. Her breath came in ragged gasps as Brooke's hand slid lower and she arched into the pleasure of Brooke's touch. She gripped the sheets beneath her, her fingers twisting in the fabric as Brooke's lips trailed down her neck, her hand guiding her to the brink. Over and over until her body trembled with release and Reggie's mind went blank, her only focus the warmth of Brooke's skin, the feel of her body intertwined with hers, and the overwhelming sense of feeling finally fulfilled.

They lay together afterward, tangled in the sheets, her body still humming with the aftershocks of pleasure. Brooke's hand rested gently on Reggie's side, her touch soft and tender, as if she never wanted to let go.

"I love you," Reggie whispered, her voice barely audible in the quiet room.

Brooke smiled, her fingers tracing light patterns on Reggie's skin. "I love you too," she whispered back, her voice steady and full of certainty.

As they lay there in the quiet, their bodies pressed close, Reggie knew that this—right here, with Brooke—was exactly where she was meant to be.

CHAPTER TWENTY-TWO

A re you saying Gloria Leland was involved in framing your brother?" Brooke was a little lost in the story the others were weaving together, partly because she hadn't been part of their shorthand from the beginning and partly because she was distracted by the very recent memory of Reggie's hands exploring every inch of her body. She glanced at Reggie who was sitting girlfriend close on the extra-long couch in Lennox's and Wren's apartment, and got a sexy, knowing smile flashed her way.

"That's exactly what I'm saying," Lennox said, pointing one finger at her and another at her own nose. "I keep forgetting you don't have all of the backstory." She shifted her focus to Reggie. "Fill your girl in, why don't you?"

Your girl. She could tell by the brightening of Reggie's eyes she liked the term and Brooke surprised herself by loving it, embracing it, whispering it to herself with the low breath of excitement.

"Don't mind Lennox," Reggie whispered against her ear. "She gets excited talking about crime."

"Seems to be a lot of that going around. The excitement part, anyway." Brooke whispered back. "And I kind of like being called your girl."

"Oh yeah?" Reggie grinned. "Well, I'm yours too, you know."

"You know, this being someone's girl definitely has some bonuses."

"Hey, lovebirds!"

They both looked up to see Lennox pointing again. Brooke turned to Reggie. "Is she always this bossy?"

"This is mild," Reggie answered. "Right, Wren?"

Wren laughed. "Hundred percent. It's one of the things I love most about her. That and the way she's going deep crimson at me being all mushy in front of people."

Lennox's blush deepened and the rest of the crowd laughed. Brooke couldn't remember ever feeling so comfortable in a big crowd of people she hardly knew, but Reggie's friends were so at ease with each other it was hard to keep up her guard. Never had she felt more at home, and the realization prompted her to join in the conversation full force. "Okay, Lennox, when you're done pretending to be embarrassed, please finish filling in the pieces, 'cause this girl needs some closure." She punctuated the declaration by squeezing Reggie's hand to let her know the closure didn't apply to her.

Lennox shot a knowing glance at them and then started in. "It started about four years ago when my brother was charged with murder in Fort Worth. Gloria Leland, Shirley Mitchell's attorney, represented him on that case and talked him into taking a plea despite the fact he didn't remember anything about what happened. He's currently serving a twenty-year sentence."

Franco, Judge Nina Aguilar's girlfriend, chimed in. "It turns out that Lennox's brother, Daniel, was framed. The murder, probably committed by one of Harry Benton's lackeys, was part of a scheme to have a section of the city condemned and later sold to Benton Enterprises. Benton hired Gloria Leland to form a fake nonprofit to petition the city to condemn the land, and then to keep the truth from coming out at trial, he bribed Gloria to represent Daniel and talk him into taking a plea. Daniel's lack of memory about what happened, likely because he'd been drugged, meant he didn't feel like he had a choice between taking twenty with a chance of release at ten or risking life in prison with a jury."

Brooke nodded, but her mind was spinning with the onslaught of information. Having narrowly escaped the long reach of Harry Benton only the day before, she had a taste of what it felt like to feel completely out of control. "Is he okay?" She looked at Lennox, "Can you get him out of prison now?"

Lennox nodded. "Thanks to Wren and Franco, Daniel has a hearing set next week for a bond pending appeal. They'll be presenting evidence to the trial judge to show the plea was coerced, and you'll never believe who one of the star witnesses will be."

Could it be Mark? Brooke shook her head. That guy was a psychopath, the perfect tool for someone as evil as Harry Benton seemed to be. No way would he testify against him. "Tell me?"

"Shirley Mitchell," Lennox announced. "Sarah and the US Attorney's office finally helped her see the light. It didn't hurt that she was appalled to hear that Benton had threatened Ben. That combined with the fact Benton had gotten close to threatening her own kids made her finally come around. And once she started talking, she spilled everything she knew which means we have solid leads to prove Benton hired the guy who shot up Nina's courtroom to cover up the fact he had his own daughter murdered."

Brooke gasped at the revelation. "His own daughter?" If Benton would have his own daughter killed, he would stop at nothing.

"It's a fact," Franco said. "He's big on arranging things to make sure his business thrives no matter who gets in the way.

When we called him on it, a few months ago, he showed up at Nina's house and threatened her to try to keep her quiet."

"True," Nina said, placing a hand on Franco's arm. "If you hadn't shown up, I'm certain either Harry or I would be dead."

"I'm glad I got there in time," Franco said. "But in a throwdown between you and Harry Benton, my money would be on you." She turned to Brooke. "Don't worry about Ben. The feds are watching Benton's every move and he'll be arrested soon."

Brooke nodded, but she couldn't manage to come up with words to express how much she appreciated everyone in this room and the lengths they'd gone to to keep her and Ben safe. Sure, they'd all had their own motivations for taking Benton down, but they'd banded together as a group to come to her aid, and the woman beside her was the reason why. She leaned over to Reggie while everyone else in the room started chiming in about what they thought and hoped would happen to Benton. "Promise me you'll fill in the gaps later when we're alone."

Reggie grinned. "Not what I had planned for our alone time, but maybe we can take a break in between…"

She slid her hand down Brooke's thigh and Brooke could feel the heat of her own blush. "Maybe. Or maybe we can just continue where we left off last night and worry about real life when we must. Come next week, I'll have to get back to work and school and I assume you'll be studying for your exam and figuring out the logistics of starting your own detective agency."

"Actually, Skye made me an offer and I'm considering taking it. I'd start by doing some skip tracing and light stuff while I study, and once I pass the exam, start working on her backlog of cases. What do you think?"

Brooke stared into Reggie's eyes, so full of excitement, and she was happy for her, though a little jealous that she didn't have her own next steps lined up. "Sounds like you have it all figured out."

Reggie grasped her hand and held tight. "I'm asking because I want you involved in the choices I make. I'm in this for the long haul, for you and Ben, and if we're going to be together, whatever I choose to do next will affect the three of us."

Brooke felt the tears form at the edge of her eyes just as Reggie reached out to touch them.

"Did I say something wrong?" Reggie asked.

She shook her head. "Not one thing. Everything about you, about us, feels so right. It's just hard to believe it's true."

Reggie's smile was big and broad, and she looked as confident as she had that first day they'd met at the courthouse. When she spoke, her voice was sure and steady and she was no longer whispering as if she wanted everyone in the room to hear. "I love you, Brooke Dawson. That's the truth, the whole truth, and nothing but the truth, and you better believe it."

After a declaration like that, how could she not? She glanced around for a moment, noticing the conversation in the rest of the room had trailed off. She could tell everyone was anxiously awaiting her response, but no one more so than the gorgeous, brave, loving woman seated next to her who gave her the confidence to speak her own truth. She took a deep breath knowing exactly what she wanted to say and not caring if everyone heard her say it.

"I love you too, Reggie Knoll. Beyond all doubt. You take that job with Skye and we'll figure out my next step together. I can't wait to have a wonderful life with you."

THE END

About the Author

Carsen Taite's goal as an author is to spin tales with plot lines as interesting as the cases she encountered in her career as a criminal defense lawyer. She is the award-winning author of over thirty novels of romance and romantic intrigue, including the Luca Bennett Bounty Hunter series, the Lone Star Law series, the Legal Affairs romances, and the Courting Danger series.

Books Available from Bold Strokes Books

Close to Home by Allisa Bahney. Eli Thomas has to decide if avoiding her hometown forever is worth losing the people who used to mean the most to her, especially Aracely Hernandez, the girl who got away. (978-1-63679-661-1)

Innis Harbor by Patricia Evans. When Amir Farzaneh meets and falls in love with Loch, a dark secret lurking in her past reappears, threatening the happiness she'd just started to believe could be hers. (978-1-63679-781-6)

The Blessed by Anne Shade. Layla and Suri are brought together by fate to defeat the darkness threatening to tear their world apart. What they don't expect to discover is a love that might set them free. (978-1-63679-715-1)

The Guardians by Sheri Lewis Wohl. Dogs, devotion, and determination are all that stand between darkness and light. (978-1-63679-681-9)

The Mogul Meets Her Match by Julia Underwood. When CEO Claire Beauchamp goes undercover as a customer of Abby Pita's café to help seal a deal that will solidify her career, she doesn't expect to be so drawn to her. When the truth is revealed, will she break Abby's heart? (978-1-63679-784-7)

Trial Run by Carsen Taite. When Reggie Knoll and Brooke Dawson wind up serving on a jury together, their one task—reaching a unanimous verdict—is derailed by the fiery clash of their personalities, the intensity of their attraction, and a secret that could threaten Brooke's life. (978-1-63555-865-4)

Waterlogged by Nance Sparks. When conservation warden Jordan Pearce discovers a body floating in the flowage, the serenity of the Northwoods is rocked. (978-1-63679-699-4)

Accidentally in Love by Kimberly Cooper Griffin. Nic and Lee have good reasons for keeping their distance. So why does their growing attraction seem more like a love-hate relationship? (978-1-63679-759-5)

Fatal Foul Play by David S. Pederson. After eight friends are stranded in an old lodge by a blinding snowstorm, a brutal murder leaves Mark Maddox to solve the crime as he discovers deadly secrets about people he thought he knew. (978-1-63679-794-6)

Frosted by the Girl Next Door by Aurora Rey and Jaime Clevenger. When heartbroken Casey Stevens opens a sex shop next door to uptight cupcake baker Tara McCoy, things get a little frosty. (978-1-63679-723-6)

Ghost of the Heart by Catherine Friend. Being possessed by a ghost was not on Gwen's bucket list, but she must admit that ghosts might be real, and one is obviously trying to send her a message. (978-1-63555-112-9)

Hot Honey Love by Nan Campbell. When chef Stef Lombardozzi puts her cooking career into the hands of filmmaker Mallory Radowski—the pickiest eater alive—she doesn't anticipate how hard she falls for her. (978-1-63679-743-4)

London by Patricia Evans. Jaq's and Bronwyn's lives become entwined as dangerous secrets emerge and Bronwyn's seemingly perfect life starts to unravel. (978-1-63679-778-6)

This Christmas by Georgia Beers. When Sam's grandmother rigs the Christmas parade to make Sam and Keegan queen and queen, sparks fly, but they can't forget the Big Embarrassing Thing that makes romance a total nope. (978-1-63679-729-8)

Unwrapped by D. Jackson Leigh. Asia du Muir is not going to let some party girl actress ruin her best chance to get noticed by a Broadway critic. Everyone knows you should never mix business and pleasure. (978-1-63679-667-3)

Language Lessons by Sage Donnell. Grace and Lenka never expected to fall in love. Is home really where the heart is if it means giving up your dreams? (978-1-63679-725-0)

New Horizons by Shia Woods. When Quinn Collins meets Alex Anders, Horizon Theater's enigmatic managing director, a passionate connection ignites, but amidst the complex backdrop of theater politics, their budding romance faces a formidable challenge. (978-1-63679-683-3)

Scrambled: A Tuesday Night Book Club Mystery by Jaime Maddox. Avery Hutchins makes a discovery about her father's death that will force her to face an impossible choice between doing what is right and finally finding a way to regain a part of herself she had lost. (978-1-63679-703-8)

Stolen Hearts by Michele Castleman. Finding the thief who stole a precious heirloom will become Ella's first move in a dangerous game of wits that exposes family secrets and could lead to her family's financial ruin. (978-1-63679-733-5)

Synchronicity by J.J. Hale. Dance, destiny, and undeniable passion collide at a summer camp as Haley and Cal navigate a love story that intertwines past scars with present desires. (978-1-63679-677-2)

The First Kiss by Patricia Evans. As the intrigue surrounding her latest case spins dangerously out of control, military police detective Parker Haven must choose between her career and the woman she's falling in love with. (978-1-63679-775-5)

Wild Fire by Radclyffe & Julie Cannon. When Olivia returns to the Red Sky Ranch, Riley's carefully crafted safe world goes up in flames. Can they take a risk and cross the fire line to find love? (978-1-63679-727-4)

Writ of Love by Cassidy Crane. Kelly and Jillian struggle to navigate the ruthless battleground of Big Law, grappling with desire, ambition, and the thin line between success and surrender. (978-1-63679-738-0)

Back to Belfast by Emma L. McGeown. Two colleagues are asked to trade jobs. Claire moves to Vancouver and Stacie moves to Belfast, and though they've never met in person, they can't seem to escape a growing attraction from afar. (978-1-63679-731-1)

Exposure by Nicole Disney and Kimberly Cooper Griffin. For photographer Jax Bailey and delivery driver Trace Logan, keeping it casual is a matter of perspective. (978-1-63679-697-0)

Hunt of Her Own by Elena Abbott. Finding forever won't be easy, but together Danaan's and Ashly's paths lead back to the supernatural sanctuary of Terabend. (978-1-63679-685-7)

Perfect by Kris Bryant. They say opposites attract, but Alix and Marianna have totally different dreams. No Hollywood love story is perfect, right? (978-1-63679-601-7)

Royal Expectations by Jenny Frame. When childhood sweethearts Princess Teddy Buckingham and Summer Fisher reunite, their feelings resurface and so does the public scrutiny that tore them apart. (978-1-63679-591-1)

Shadow Rider by Gina L. Dartt. In the Shadows, one can easily find death, but can Shay and Keagan find love as they fight to save the Five Nations? (978-1-63679-691-8)

The Breakdown by Ronica Black. Vaughn and Natalie have chemistry, but the outside world keeps knocking at the door, threatening more trouble, making the love and the life they want together impossible. (978-1-63679-675-8)

Tribute by L.M. Rose. To save her people, Fiona will be the tribute in a treaty marriage to the Tipruii princess, Simaala, and spend the rest of her days on the other side of the wall between their races. (978-1-63679-693-2)

Wild Wales by Patricia Evans. When Finn and Aisling fall in love, they must decide whether to return to the safety of the lives they had, or take a chance on wild love in windswept Wales. (978-1-63679-771-7)